The Austen Sisters

The Austen Sisters

A Modern Day Tale of Pride, Persuasion, and Sensibilities

DEE BLANKENSHIP

First edition

ISBN 979-8-9920803-0-8 (paperback)

ISBN 979-8-9920803-3-9 (hardcover)

ISBN 979-8-9920803-1-5 (ebook)

"A sister is a little bit of childhood that can never be lost."
-Marion C. Garretty

For my sisters, Gabriella Kennedy-Law,
Toni Pisaneschi, Danielle Kennedy, and Rebecca Broussard,
the strongest, funniest, fiercest women I know.

And for my Mum, Ellen Kennedy, my biggest cheerleader
and best friend.
I always said I would, because you always said I could.

PROLOGUE

No one who had ever met the Austen sisters would have presumed them to be heroines of a novel.

Unless of course, they have read Jane Austen.

The eldest of the five sisters, Elinor Austen, is possessed with all the qualities expected of an older sister. She is reserved, pragmatic, protective, and occasionally judgmental, just ask her sisters. At thirty-one, she is completely focused on her career over any prospects of marriage. But a recent project with a new colleague has our heroine questioning whether to follow her sense or finally give in to her well-contained sensibilities.

Our next heroine, with her charm and humor, may easily be the most popular of the sisters. Elizabeth Austen is full of sparkle and wit but let us not overlook her faults. Her passion and pride can lead her to false impressions and prejudices. She has turned her lifelong passion for reading into a career in publishing, finding happiness working for a small company specializing in romantic fiction. Elizabeth is good at reading romance novels, but can she find love outside the pages of a book?

In a family of five, there must always be a middle child, and Anne Austen holds that position. Neither particularly beautiful nor notably witty, she appreciates that she is suited to the role of a wallflower. But Anne's sympathetic nature and calm counsel is the heart of the family. She has chosen her path at the persuasion of others and must now figure out how to follow her own mind and heart.

Is there not always one heroine who seems to have it all? Emma Austen has the self-assuredness that comes with beauty and the wit that comes with being clever. At twenty-three, she has carved out a niche in the world of social media. Her latest project is the launch of a dating app. While she isn't searching for love herself, she's dedicated to helping others find it. Will our heroines misapplied sense lead to love...or mischief?

Catherine Austen is the most unlikely of heroines. She is naive to the world around her, but what she lacks in experience she makes up for in kindness. She is, as all baby sisters are, spoiled by her older siblings and much beloved. But do not misinterpret her naivety for lack of intelligence. Our heroine must simply learn to pull her head out of her book and seek the adventures that should befall all young ladies.

You are cordially invited
to the wedding of

Fanny Price

&

Edmund Bertram

Saturday the fourteenth of June, two thousand twenty-five
four o'clock in the afternoon
at

Mansfield Park

CHAPTER I

Elinor

"Sense will always have attractions for me."

- SENSE AND SENSIBILITY

Elinor caught sight of the gate for her flight and let out a sigh of relief. Flying itself didn't bother her, once she was on the plane, she was fine. It was everything leading up to it that made her anxious: the traffic, the parking, the long security lines. That was the real stress. For at least the tenth time, she patted her carry-on pockets, double checking that her boarding pass and driver's license were still there. Finally, sliding into the airport lounge chair, she let herself relax for the first time all morning.

It was finally sinking in. She was going on vacation! The past few months had been a nonstop blur of meetings, pitches and deadlines. Now, as she looked ahead to a week of festivities, she realized how unprepared she was. But what a week it promised to be.

Fanny's wedding! The wedding of her younger cousin to Edmund Bertram was going to be a grand affair. The Bertrams were a wealthy, old-money Kentucky family.

The family's wealth traced back to their early success in tobacco farming. Over the years they had expanded into real estate and thoroughbred racing. The Bertram name was now synonymous with old money and influence. Fanny and Edmund's wedding promised to be one of the biggest events of the summer, held at one of Kentucky's most luxurious resorts. And not only would Elinor and her sisters be attending, but, as Fanny's closest family, they were also to be her bridesmaids. The whole thing felt a bit surreal.

She picked up her phone, opened the group chat with her sisters, and sent off a quick text:

I'm at the airport! Can't wait to see you all soon!!

Her sister Elizabeth immediately responded.

Sooo, how early are you? I bet your plane isn't even on the runway yet.

Elinor glanced out the airport window, noticing through the fog that her plane wasn't on the tarmac. She let out a deep sigh. She would *not* be confirming this fact for her sister.

The next text came from Emma.

Just please tell me you aren't wearing a fanny pack!

Geez, just one time—one time!—and you never live it down, Elinor mumbled to herself. She furiously typed back,

I am most definitely NOT wearing a fanny pack, thank you very much!

Elinor pictured Emma's long, manicured nails flying across the keys as her next message popped up:

Let me guess, it's a cross-body?

Elinor groaned and subconsciously pulled her cross-body purse closer. She missed the teasing and banter of her sisters, but she also wondered how they could so easily get to the heart of her own insecurities. And what was so wrong with dressing practically anyway?

For the first time, she gave some thought to what she was wearing. Taking in her "sensible shoes," as Emma would call them, and her cross-body purse, which she would now be hiding in her luggage before her sisters saw it, she sighed. How on Earth was she going to fit into the Bertrams' world of lavish parties, wealthy socialites, and designer fashion?

For that matter, how were any of her sisters going to fit in? Nestled among the horse farms of eastern Kentucky, Mansfield Park Resort was luxury beyond their wildest dreams. An opulent hotel with gardens and a golf course, Mansfield was considered one of the country's most upscale resorts. It was only because of the Bertrams' generous offer to pay for the sisters' stay that they were even able to make the trip.

Emma sent another text.

Since you've apparently got lots of time to kill, don't forget to create a profile on my app! Resending the link so you have it handy. See you soon, sis!

Elinor rolled her eyes and felt a pang of annoyance. Emma had sent the link several times already. She couldn't believe her sister was actually promoting a dating app, of all things. Emma, who claimed she was never going to fall in love, was now actually trying to get others to fall into it. The irony was not lost on Elinor.

Anne chimed in next.

I confirmed our reservation with the resort. We have two adjoining suites with garden views! Whoever checks in first, be sure to pick up the week's itinerary. Can't wait to see you all.

Elinor smiled. She loved that she could count on Anne's efficiency to keep them all organized. It took some of the pressure off herself.

The last text was from her youngest sister, Catherine.

OMG cant wait the FOMO is REAL!!! I have one more exam (sad face emoji) then I'll be on my way (happy face emoji) can't wait to see you guys (followed by ten heart emojis)

Elinor studied Catherine's text and sighed. Didn't they still teach grammar in college? Ten years separated the two sisters, and sometimes Elinor cringed at her youngest sister's exuberance. And what the hell was FOMO anyway?

As the oldest of the five sisters, Elinor carried a tremendous sense of duty to her siblings. When their mother passed away—Elinor was nineteen and Catherine merely nine—all the sisters developed a tight-knit bond. They had slowly watched their father disappear into his grief, and although he loved his daughters, he failed miserably at raising them. That burden had fallen on Elinor.

Their father's death a few years later compounded their loss, leaving Elinor to shoulder even more responsibility.

She was fiercely protective of her sisters but also set high expectations for them. She had strongly encouraged them to pursue their education, determined that they would achieve financial independence without depending on anyone else. Although they occasionally resented their eldest sister's involvement, her efforts had been worthwhile. Elinor now took great pride in their accomplishments.

Elizabeth had embarked on a promising career in book editing, Anne was preparing to begin graduate school, and Catherine was completing her third year of college.

She sighed. And Emma...Emma was the only one who gave Elinor cause for concern.

Emma had always found it difficult to accept Elinor's authority. When Emma decided to drop out of college to pursue "social media ventures," Elinor suspected the decision was made to spite her. Emma's seamless entry into the social media world and transformation into a minor celebrity "influencer" left Elinor feeling puzzled.

While texting often with all the sisters, Elinor relied on Emma's prolific Instagram posts to stay updated on her sister's life. Constantly posting to promote new trends or products, Emma had recently been sharing stories about her new dating app, encouraging followers to sign up and find their one true love.

Elinor couldn't hold back her disapproval; she was certain that Emma couldn't earn a living through social media.

Following their mother's passing, Elinor had opted for a local community college instead of a prestigious art school, choosing to prioritize the care of her sisters, particularly the younger ones. Although she didn't regret her choices, she felt that Emma didn't fully appreciate what she had sacrificed.

It was only over the past few years that she felt her sisters had finally reached a point of stability. For the first time in her life, Elinor felt she could focus on her own goals and aspirations. Choosing to accept a position with a publishing firm as a children's book illustrator was a dream come true. But relocating from her small hometown in Kentucky to the bustling city of Chicago was the hardest decision she'd ever faced.

Now it had been nearly two years since she last saw her sisters. Though she was looking forward to her cousin's wedding, she was even more thrilled at the prospect of reuniting with them. As much as they drove her crazy, she really missed them.

Her phone pinged again with a notification; she glanced at it expecting another text from one of her sisters. But her heart beat faster as she caught the name on her screen. Eddie.

Be practical Elinor, she chided herself. Edin Faris, was after all, merely another client, an author she was partnering with on his latest book.

He knew she was going on vacation and likely needed something urgently before her departure. So why was she feeling like a schoolgirl with her first high school crush?

She glanced anxiously down at his text.

Have a fantastic vacation, Elinor. It won't be the same

without you this week.

A smile spread across her lips.

It won't be the same without you. She tried not to read too much into his words, but it felt an awful lot like saying, *I'll miss you...*

***

By the time Elinor boarded the plane, it felt like she had been at the airport forever. She rammed her carry-on into the overhead compartment and glanced down forlornly.

Ugh. She hated being stuck in the middle seat.

What were the chances she could avoid small talk with other passengers? She relished having some downtime to relax after the hectic past few weeks.

She glanced at the man occupying the window seat, relieved to see that he was engrossed in his phone and oblivious to his surroundings. Unfortunately, the same could not be said for the woman on the aisle, who eagerly caught Elinor's eye and beamed a ruddy-cheeked smile.

Rats, thought Elinor, wishing she could channel some of Elizabeth's intimidation or Emma's indifference. But instead, she found herself giving the woman a kind smile and nod.

"Oh, I was *so* hoping I would have someone to talk to on the flight! You know it makes the trip go much faster when you have someone to chat with, don't you agree, Thomas?"

At this, she leaned forward and looked over at the gentleman in the window seat. He didn't acknowledge her glance, but Elinor could have sworn she heard him mutter the word "No" under his breath.

Unfazed, her chatty new friend continued to ramble on as Elinor squeezed in front of her to take the middle seat.

"If you two are together, I'd be more than happy to

switch seats," Elinor offered hopefully.

"Oh, heavens no, dear. We're married. Why would we want to sit together?" the woman replied, looking genuinely puzzled. "I'm Charlotte Palmer, by the way." She extended a plump hand. "And pay no mind to Mr. Palmer over there. He's perfectly happy to scroll on his phone and occasionally doze off."

At that moment, Elinor couldn't decide who she felt more sympathy for: the lively, cheerful woman married to a rude, uncouth husband, or the man who had to endure the endless chatter and tiresome ramblings of his wife. All she knew was that, given the choice of the two, she would have preferred the company of the husband for the flight.

Mrs. Palmer continued, "We are heading to visit my mother. The poor dear isn't able to fly anymore, and we've been so busy we haven't been able to get out there to see her. I just know she will be thrilled to see us." Again, she leaned across Elinor to look at Mr. Palmer. "Positively thrilled, don't you agree, Thomas?"

He didn't look up, but Elinor heard him mutter the word "Ecstatic."

"Yes, ecstatic. Exactly," said Mrs. Palmer, nodding in agreement, as if her husband had offered up some sage advice.

Elinor settled in with a smile and nodded politely as her new friend rambled on amiably about her life.

She wasn't sure when exactly she'd zoned out, but she suddenly realized Mrs. Palmer was looking at her expectantly.

"Did you hear me, dear? Here I've been rambling on about myself, and I realize I haven't asked you a single question! Where are you heading off to?"

Elinor snapped back to attention and replied, "Oh, sorry. My cousin is getting married this weekend. I'm flying out for the wedding, and my sisters and I will be her bridesmaids." She surprised herself at offering up so much information.

"Oh, I just adore weddings," Mrs. Palmer cooed and clapped her hands excitedly, as if she, too, would be attending. "Where is the ceremony?"

Elinor hesitated a little. "It's going to be at the Mansfield Park Resort."

Mrs. Palmer's eyes flew open, and she let out a sharp exclamation of surprise, one so loud it caused several other passengers to glance back at the commotion.

"Mansfield Park! Thomas, did you hear that! She's going to Mansfield Park!"

Elinor didn't need to glance at him to hear the droll, one-word reply: "Thrilling."

"Oh yes, that is thrilling! My dear, is your cousin famous? Mr. Palmer and I know several celebrities quite well, don't we, Thomas?"

Elinor wasn't sure whether to take his loud sigh as acknowledgment or disagreement, but Mrs. Palmer continued unfazed.

"We met that delightful actor who drove the talking car. Oh, what was his name?" She glanced searchingly over at her husband.

Elinor tried to hide her surprise when he actually replied. "David Hasselhoff," he said, glancing up sternly, but just momentarily, from his phone.

"Oh yes, how could I forget that!" she said, leaning in closer to Elinor. "I remember that Thomas admonished me for asking for an autograph. 'Don't hassle the Hoff,' he told me." She cackled and clapped her hands, as if hearing the joke for the first time. "Anyway, I always wonder who those people are that can stay at places like that! And here I am sitting next to one. Yes, definitely thrilling!" She continued to beam with excitement.

Elinor couldn't help but smile at Mrs. Palmer's enthusiastic response. She was certainly *not* one of those people who could afford to stay at Mansfield Park. She had been overwhelmed by the Bertrams' generous offer to pay for the sisters' rooms at the resort for the four nights leading up to and including the wedding day. She had only reluctantly accepted their offer when Fanny insisted she needed her cousins by her side for her special day.

The topic of weddings had set Mrs. Palmer off anew. Now she was going on about her own wedding to the "charming and funny" Mr. Palmer.

Elinor smiled and nodded as encouragement, but she once again allowed her thoughts to wander, not to the upcoming wedding, but to a pair of dark, soulful eyes that belonged to one Edin Faris.

CHAPTER 2

Elizabeth

"I could easily forgive his pride, if he had not mortified mine."

- PRIDE AND PREJUDICE

Elizabeth fumed as she randomly stuffed clothes into her suitcase. *You're just not my type.* Those were the exact words he'd used. The nerve of him! Just who did he think he was? Well, just so it was clear, *he* wasn't her type either! Okay well, maybe tall, broad-shouldered, sharply dressed, and devastatingly handsome, with deep, chocolate brown eyes *was* her type. But all that was lost with his arrogant, boorish, rude smugness—and she could probably come up with more infuriatingly annoying traits if she weren't still so angry.

So why was she still thinking about him and his stupid comment? Best to just put the whole horrible date out of her mind and focus on the job at hand, packing for a dream vacation. She glanced down at the items she had thrown into her suitcase: T-shirts, jeans, a few sweatshirts. She let out a sigh. It looked like she was packing for a camping trip, not a week at a luxurious resort. The week ahead promised to be amazing. Fanny and Edmund were getting married! Not only was she beyond excited for her cousin, but she was also getting a much-needed vacation *and* an opportunity to see all her sisters. She simply couldn't wait.

A grand hotel amid the rolling hills of Kentucky, complete with a golf course, spa, brewery, and famous gardens. The thought of hanging around a bunch of wealthy social snobs didn't appeal to her, but as long as she had her sisters and Fanny, she didn't really care who else was there.

She set the directions on her phone. It was a three-hour drive from Indianapolis to the Kentucky resort. That was plenty of time to clear her head of last night's disastrous date and think about more pleasant things, like a week of drowning in absolute luxury.

But ten minutes into the drive, she found herself on the phone, calling her sister Anne for advice.

"This is all Emma's fault," Elizabeth complained. "I absolutely can't believe I let her talk me into using her dating app!"

"Surely it's not as bad as all that? How bad could a date go?" Anne asked patiently.

That was all the prompting Elizabeth needed. She immediately launched into the details of last night's date.

Emma's app was designed to match couples who'd picked the same location for their first date. Elizabeth thought the idea was pretty cool. She immediately knew which spot she was going to pick. The place was called The Book Club, a literary-themed cocktail bar decorated like a cozy library. It was a new hot spot amid downtown's nightlife and drew in a young crowd. She had been dying to check the place out, but, seeing as she was very single at the moment, going with a date had seemed out of the question.

Creating a profile had been more fun than she thought, and she was pleasantly surprised when she got a quick response from a potential match. From his profile picture, he looked a little more serious than the type of guy she'd normally go out with. And his profile was light on details. She hadn't been able to glean much from his feed except that he also worked in the publishing industry. And if the pic was real, he was very, very good-looking.

Since the bar was only four blocks from her office, she had opted to walk rather than order an Uber. But she had misjudged the distance and the weather.

"How late were you?" Anne interjected at this point.

Elizabeth sighed. "Not very, maybe twenty minutes, tops. I mean, I wouldn't have been late at all if it hadn't started to rain."

"Did you have an umbrella?" Anne interjected again.

"No, but really, is that an important question right now?" Elizabeth asked, exasperated by her sister's interruptions. It dawned on her that she might have called more to rant rather than to get advice.

"Well, if you didn't have an umbrella and you walked in the rain, I'm just saying that you probably didn't look your best. You know how your hair gets frizzy when it's wet," Anne said simply.

"The point is the date was awful, not that my hair was frizzy," Elizabeth said, rolling her eyes and subconsciously tucking a strand of hair behind her ear.

"Well, I'm just saying first impressions matter," Anne offered up helpfully.

"Can I finish my story?" Elizabeth grumbled impatiently. "I haven't even told you how terrible he was yet."

Anne laughed. "Okay, but you need to hurry up. I'm

driving, too, and I'm almost there."

Elizabeth launched back into her story with gusto. The rain had caught her off guard, and without an umbrella her normally soft brown locks were frizzy and untamed. To top it off, her pant legs were mud stained and wet. Not really the look she was going for, but nothing could be done about it at this point. She immediately recognized Darcy Fitzwilliam from his profile on the app, and her heart had skipped a beat. Damn, he was even better looking in person. They caught each other's eye, and she smiled and waved. He returned neither. She hastily approached the table, and he stood up to greet her. She wouldn't consider herself short at five-seven, but he towered over her. She guessed he had to be at least six-three. He was impeccably dressed in a tailored suit fitted perfectly to his broad shoulders. He had dark black hair, thick dark brows, and light brown eyes that softened some of his harsher features, but they glared at Elizabeth with such intensity that she shrank back from his gaze. Still, despite the deep scowl, he was unquestionably attractive.

"Darcy?" she asked, trying not to sound as winded as she felt from her walk. "I'm Elizabeth. I'm so sorry for keeping you waiting."

"You're out of breath. Did you...did you walk here?" he asked a little incredulously. "In the rain?"

Elizabeth let out a joyful laugh. "I did. I enjoy walking, but I was a little off on the timing and the weather. Again, I'm sorry I kept you waiting. But check this place out," she said, taking off her jacket and looking around at the bar's decor.

The walls featured portraits of famous writers, quotes, and lots of bookshelves. She noticed the quote above their table was from *Jane Eyre*; "Reader, I married him" hung on the wall above Darcy's head. She smiled to herself. Maybe a good omen? Then her eyes returned to his scowling face.

Then again, maybe not.

She glanced down at the drink menu, delighted at the book-themed drinks: The Turning of the Screwdriver, Gone with the Gin, and Pitchers of Dorian Gray.

"Well, this is fun! What should we start with?" she said, trying to relax and break the ice.

Darcy arched a disapproving eyebrow and glanced down at his watch. "It's late, and I've got a long drive tomorrow. I'd prefer to just order the food," he said, a full frown replacing the slight scowl.

They sat in silence while they waited for their food. Elizabeth, growing more uncomfortable, was relieved when the waitress arrived with their plates. Darcy finally cleared his throat and asked her a question.

"Your profile stated you are a book editor. Which publishing house do you work for?" He didn't make eye contact, just focused intently on the plate of food in front of him.

She smiled, pleased that he'd taken the time to read her profile. "I work for Charlotte Lucas Publishing here in downtown Indianapolis," she said proudly. It was a small firm, but she loved being part of a small tight knit and passionate community.

"Don't they primarily publish romance novels?" he asked, seeming to really look at her for the first time.

Elizabeth responded enthusiastically, "Oh, good, you've heard of it? Yes, we primarily publish romantic fiction."

Darcy looked at her with a disapproving stare, and she wondered if he had any other facial expression.

She felt a little flush of anger. "Let me guess, I bet you're one of those who only reads the classics. Do you have a problem with romantic fiction?" she asked defensively.

"I do, actually." He scoffed but appeared to relax a bit. "It's just the same overused tropes. Enemies to lovers, second chance romance, the grand gesture; it's just all so predictable and repetitive. I find it quite boring," he said tightly.

Elizabeth tried to contain her irritation. "I disagree. I think romance offers readers a chance to escape their daily lives, to immerse themselves in a world of passion and love, and I don't see anything wrong with that."

"You don't think it sets unrealistic expectations for women?" Darcy replied, this time catching her eyes with a penetrating stare. "Implying that marriage is a woman's only way to happiness? You're a career woman yourself; I'm surprised you're not offended by such an antiquated notion." The intensity of his gaze disarmed her a bit.

"I don't think encouraging women to enter into healthy relationships that bring them fulfillment is an antiquated notion," she asserted, a little too defensively. "Plus, I think everyone deserves their HEA."

At this, Darcy arched an eyebrow, which Elizabeth tried not to find so attractive as it diffused some of her anger.

"HEA. What is HEA?" asked Darcy, truly puzzled.

"You know, happily ever after," she said with exasperation.

"Hmm, so setting unrealistic expectations for women to believe that if they find the right one, life will be perfect?" he asked in earnest. "I mean, how many people really get their happily ever after?"

"I think you are misconstruing what happily ever after means," she said, her voice rising with passion. "It's not some Cinderella notion that you will be happy every day if you only find the handsome prince. It's about finding that person who makes you a better version of yourself, who sees you as you truly are, who encourages you to be better, to do better." She was on a roll now. "It is about recognizing that life is going to throw all kinds of challenges at you and finding the person you want to face those challenges with." She stared back at him, trying to read the expression in his eyes.

"I just think you are raising expectations. The chances that most of us will find that one person are low," he replied, his voice much softer now.

"Hmph," replied Elizabeth. "Well, perhaps you aren't looking in the right places."

A few minutes of silence ensued before Elizabeth tried again at conversation.

"So I'm guessing your firm doesn't publish romance, where exactly do you work?" she asked, hoping they could get back to some common ground, click over their mutual love of books, anything to turn this date around.

He cleared his throat and replied, "I work at Pemberley Publishing."

Elizabeth paused, her fork halfway to her mouth. *Wow, Pemberley.*

Pemberley Publishing was every book editor's dream job. They hired only the best and brightest, and it was synonymous with quality literature. Working for Pemberley meant Darcy was probably making *a lot* of money. But Pemberley was also known for its tyrannical publishing director, Catherine de Bourgh. Her reputation was legendary in the industry. Her cutting remarks and blunt feedback were rumored to have left grown men and women in tears.

"So what's it like working for a Miranda Priestly?" Elizabeth asked, genuinely curious.

"Miranda Priestly? I'm sorry, I don't know who that is," Darcy said, giving her a quizzical look, which, for a few moments, replaced the scowl.

"Oh, come on, really? You haven't heard that before?" she asked in disbelief. *The Devil Wears Prada?* Meryl Streep? Surely you've heard the comparison made to your boss. She has a reputation for being a real bi—"

Before Elizabeth could finish her sentence, Darcy cut

in, "I assume you are referring to Catherine?" he asked, his dark eyes glaring at Elizabeth.

"You are on a first-name basis with Ms. de Bourgh? Impressive." she replied, trying not to sound smug but failing miserably.

"Actually, I'm more comfortable calling her Aunt Cathy rather than Catherine," he said, and for the first time all night, the hint of a smile played out on his face.

"Aunt Catherine? Catherine de Bourgh is your aunt?" Elizabeth asked shocked.

"She is," Darcy replied curtly.

Could I be a bigger idiot? Elizabeth thought, hearing Chandler Bing's voice echo in her head. She fully expected Darcy to rub it in or respond gleefully, but his reply was just matter of fact. He cleared his throat and continued, "My grandfather founded the firm. Catherine is now the oldest member of my family, and she's carrying on the business. It will pass to me at some point in the future."

Are you freaking kidding me? Elizabeth wanted to crawl under the table. His family OWNS Pemberley Publishing! Darcy would one day run Pemberley.

She took in his appearance with greater detail; the perfectly tailored navy suit, the silk tie, the expensive watch. Holy crap. Darcy wasn't just well-off; he was *really* rich.

Dinner ended the way it had started, in strained silence, and Elizabeth was more than ready for the night to be over. Not for the first time that evening, she wondered how she had let Emma talk her into signing up for a dating app. She was just on the verge of saying goodbye when Darcy cleared his throat.

Please, please, please don't ask for a second date, she thought to herself.

"Look, I really don't want to waste either of our time, and I think it's clear this isn't going to work out, so I think it's best that we leave it at this one date. Honestly, you're just not my type."

Elizabeth flushed with embarrassment. *Not his type?* What did that even mean? She wasn't rich enough for him? Her job wasn't prestigious enough? He didn't find her attractive? Ugh, the nerve of this man! As far as she was concerned, she couldn't get away from him fast enough. She tried to maintain her dignity as she hurriedly grabbed her purse and jacket, mustering the last of her courage to give a sweet smile and murmur, "Good luck finding your happily ever after, Darcy."

She finished up her story to Anne feeling a smug satisfaction that she was in the right.

"I mean, like, what the hell, Anne? He couldn't just say, *Well, nice to meet you,* or, *Have a good life,* or, *Sorry, my social calendar is pretty booked*—which, by the way, I'm pretty sure it's *not*! No, he has to tell me I'm *not his type?* What does that even mean?"

"Well, you did insult his relative," Anne said with a laugh.

"Really, Anne? You're supposed to be on my side!" Elizabeth huffed.

"Okay, sorry, you're right. He sounds beastly, and it's his loss for sure. But if I were you, I'd be more worried about what you're going to tell Emma when you don't have anything to post on her app."

Elizabeth groaned. "I know, she's going to kill me."

A sudden gasp from Anne startled her.

"What? What's going on?" Elizabeth asked, concerned.

"Lizzy, I just arrived at Mansfield, and whoa! This place is going to be amazing. You need to hurry up and get here."

CHAPTER 3

Anne

"She was only Anne."

- Persuasion

Anne ended the call with her sister right as she pulled up to the Mansfield Park Resort. Nestled amidst rolling hills and lush greenery, the resort exuded an aura of timeless elegance.

She followed the signs to the resort's parking lot, driving past the man-made lake, complete with a bridge and waterfall. Vine-covered arbors lined the driveway, and in the distance she could see just catch a glimpse of the famed Mansfield Gardens.

It was as if she'd just driven into a regency romance novel.

She could almost see Fanny walking along the path in her wedding dress, a vision that sent a pang of envy through Anne. *Always the bridesmaid, never the bride*, as the saying went, though in her case, even that wasn't quite true. Until now, she had never been a bridesmaid either. It was strange, really, that not a single Austen sister had yet to get married. Although, there was that one time Elizabeth had received a marriage proposal after just one date. Anne giggled recalling her sister's horror at the odd offer.

Elinor, thirty-one, and Elizabeth, twenty-nine, had never even had a serious boyfriend she could think of. Anne was puzzled by her sisters' focus on their careers, wondering if marriage ever crossed their minds. She, on the other hand, thought about it all the time.

Unlike her older sisters, she'd received a serious proposal, one she would have accepted if she'd listened to her heart. But she had been persuaded to choose a different path. Now, she frequently wished she could turn back time and choose differently.

Anne chided herself to shake off this feeling of melancholy and just let herself be happy for Fanny. She *was* happy for Fanny, very happy that her cousin was marrying her childhood sweetheart. But deep down she couldn't help but wonder if her own turn would ever come.

She pulled into the guest parking lot, scanning the rows of expensive cars. A wave of nerves struck her, her beat-up Honda adorned with bumper stickers was bound to stick out. Ok, maybe 'adorned' was a bit of an exaggeration. It only had one sticker, placed as a joke by Elizabeth. It originally read *"Librarians do it quietly,"* but Anne, mortified, tried to peel it off and only ended up scratching the car. Now it simply read *"Librarians do it,"* which she thought was somehow worse than if she'd just left it alone.

She pulled in between a Rolls-Royce and a Ferrari. It was hard to believe that Fanny would soon be a part of all this wealth.

The Bertram family was well connected, not just in business but in politics. The wedding guest list was certain to include a lot of powerful people who'd take advantage of the social setting to network and connect. Anne kept herself well informed on society and politics, and she was mildly curious who would be in attendance.

She stepped into the afternoon heat and looked out across the vast parking lot to the resort lobby. *Good grief, this place is bigger than Disneyland*, she thought. She opened her trunk and struggled to pull out her heavy suitcase. It landed hard against the ground and smashed into the pavement, knocking off one of the wheels. *You've got to be kidding me.* She grimaced, forced now to carry her suitcase across the parking lot.

The summer heat felt brutal. *Why do brides always pick June for their weddings?* she wondered, trying to free up a hand to wipe her brow. When she got married, it would definitely be a fall wedding, complete with autumn foliage, pumpkins and hot apple cider cocktails. Anne smiled to herself at the image of her ideal wedding day.

Her daydream was interrupted when she finally entered the air-conditioned lobby.

The resort hummed with guests checking in, and she suddenly became very self-conscious of her appearance. Perfectly manicured women wore high heels, dresses, and designer bags, and here she was, face flushed with heat, hair damp from humidity—and she was pretty sure she had sweat stains under her arms.

"Anne! Anne Austen is that you?" a woman's soft Southern drawl called out to her.

Anne cringed. Who could she possibly know here other than one of her sisters? But she looked up to see the groom's sisters, Julia and Mariah Bertram.

Julia was the youngest of Edmund's sisters. She wore her hair in a sleek bob and her dress perfectly tailored— Anne was pretty sure it was designer. She started to lean in to give Anne a hug but seemed to think better of it. "Oh my god! Look at you, Anne Austen, you haven't changed one bit. I think those are even the same glasses you were wearing the last time we saw you."

Anne subconsciously pushed her glasses up her nose. For the record, they were *not* the same glasses. They were new, just the same style.

It had probably been ten years since she had seen any of the Bertrams. The last summer they'd spent with Fanny was when Anne was fifteen. She suddenly remembered why she had disliked those summers so much. For Anne, who was already a shy and insecure girl, hanging around Fanny's wealthy neighbors, the popular and pretty Bertram sisters, had been sheer torture.

Despite the insecurity Julia's appearance instilled in her, Mariah intensified those feelings significantly. Taller than both Anne and Julia, and even more elegantly dressed, she carried herself with an air of sophistication and haughtiness.

Julia continued, "I just couldn't believe it when Edmund told me you and your sisters were to be Fanny's bridesmaids. Poor Fanny. She always had a hard time making friends, didn't she?" Julia had tried to sound sympathetic but Anne didn't think she quite pulled it off.

"Good thing she can count on family," Mariah said, smiling sweetly, and Anne remembered vividly why she had never liked Mariah in particular.

"Oh, did you know Mariah is engaged too? You probably saw it on social media." Julia didn't wait for Anne's response before she turned to her sister. "Go on, Mariah; show her the ring." Turning back to Anne, Julia said, "It's simply to die for."

For the first time, Mariah smiled, thrusting out her hand, which was adorned with the largest diamond Anne had ever seen.

"It's three carats," she said, pulling back her own hand to admire it herself.

Anne gave obligatory remarks about its size and beauty but couldn't help thinking it was garish. The type of ring worn to signify status, not love. Not at all the type of ring Anne wanted when she got engaged.

"Two weddings for the family, how wonderful. Your parents must be very happy," Anne said, hoping she sounded more genuine than she felt.

"Yes, but mine is going to be a destination wedding. We are thinking of Italy, or maybe France," Mariah said, still gazing down at her ring.

"How exciting for you. I look forward to meeting him this week," Anne said cheerfully.

Mariah gave a frown and replied quickly, "No, I'm afraid not. James is at a convention this week. He won't be able to make it." Anne thought she detected relief, not disappointment, in Mariah's face.

At that moment, Mariah caught sight of another guest and yelled out excitedly, "JW! Over here!"

Anne turned to find a tall, rugged looking man making his way toward them. His slow, easy stride gave him a relaxed carefree manner.

"Well, hot damn! If it ain't the beautiful Bertram sisters," he said, giving both Mariah and Julia an appraising look, then nodding quickly at Anne. "Morning, ladies," he said as he swiped off his hat. His black hair was tousled and unkempt underneath. If the accent hadn't given it away, the cowboy hat and boots would definitely have tipped her off to his Texas roots.

"Howdy," Julia said eagerly, smiling up at him.

Mariah shot her sister a contemptuous look. "Really, Julia? *Howdy*? We aren't at a rodeo."

Julia shrank back, embarrassed by her sister's reproach, and for the first time, Anne felt just a teensy bit sorry for her.

Mariah, somewhat indifferent, made the introduction. "Anne, this is John Willoughby, one of my brother's groomsmen. John, this is one of Fanny's cousins. Our father is generously paying for their stay this week." Her words were polite but Anne could see no reason for Mariah's final remark, other than a deliberate attempt to embarrass her.

JW leaned forward. "Only my dad and the law call me John Willoughby. To everyone else, it's just JW," he said with a wink, and his effortless charm and bright smile put Anne at ease for the first time all day. But his attention was quickly diverted when he caught sight of a woman who had just entered the lobby. He let out a low whistle. "Well I'll be! Who's that fine young lady?"

Julia, Mariah, and Anne turned toward the tall, gorgeous blond making her way over to them. She wore a beautiful peach dress that flowed with her as she walked, and she moved through the room with an effortless grace. Her upswept hair gave her an added air of elegance. The woman looked vaguely familiar to Anne, who couldn't quite place how she knew her.

Mariah, who'd been so reserved and short with Anne, now gushed, "Caroline! How wonderful to see you!"

Caroline leaned over and gave both Mariah and Julia a quick kiss on the cheek. She gave JW a cursory glance and tiny smile and then her piercing eyes landed on Anne.

"Honey, you look hotter than the Georgia summer with no shade, bless your heart," she said, giving Anne's appearance a critical once-over. She shifted her attention back to the sisters, seemingly finished acknowledging Anne

Julia made the introduction this time. "Caroline, this is Anne Austen, one of Fanny's cousins and bridesmaids. Anne, this is Caroline Bingley. I'm sure you recognize her from her modeling and acting work. Her memoir, *The Accomplished Woman* is everywhere right now, you simply must pick up a copy." Julia flashed an admiring look at Caroline. "Anyway, she's a good friend of the family and isn't it so exciting that she'll be here for Fanny's wedding?"

Anne could hardly believe her luck—or lack of it. Of

all moments to meet the most famous celebrity she'd ever seen, it had to be now, when she was a complete disaster. "Nice to meet you," she said, giving Caroline a nod rather than offering her still sweaty hand. But Caroline had already lost interest and her attention turned elsewhere.

"Julia, Mariah, dears, sorry to have kept you waiting, but we really must go. I'll wait for you by the valet," Caroline said and walked off briskly.

Mariah hurried after her without saying goodbye, and JW quickly followed.

Julia, at least, had the appearance of embarrassment on their behalf and turned back to Anne as she said, "We really are excited you're here."

Anne wasn't entirely sure it was sincere, but she at least appreciated the effort.

"I better go catch up. But honey, you really should go freshen up—you are really red! Like an overripe tomato." Then she gave a little giggle and turned to follow her sister.

Anne let out a sigh of relief as they walked off. She suddenly remembered the nickname they had given to Julia and Mariah when they were kids: the Cinderella sisters. She felt a pang of sympathy for her cousin. Was this what she was going to have to put up with from here on out, living and dealing with snobs like Edmund's own sisters?

Poor Fanny. Anne only had to brace herself for the week ahead, but Fanny was marrying into this.

Just when she thought she was home free, Anne turned and caught the gaze of a gentleman staring at her. "Gentleman" was the first word that came to her mind… that, and the fact that he was absurdly handsome. Unlike JW, there wasn't a hair out of place. He was dressed impeccably, in crisp white linen pants and a colorful guayabera shirt. His light eyes had a mischievous twinkle.

"Were those the Bertram sisters you were just talking

to?" His voice was smooth and confident. "Are you here for the Bertram wedding too?" he asked, his keen eyes full of interest.

"Yes. I've known Edmund and his sisters since we were kids, and the bride-to-be is my cousin. I'm Anne Austen. My sisters and I are her bridesmaids." Anne felt a little thrill at being able to say that. It validated her being here and gave her a sense of belonging...despite the fact that she felt so out of place.

"Will Elliot, at your service," he said, giving her a quick, playful bow. "Well, Anne, it sounds like we'll be seeing more of each other this week. JW and I are groomsmen. It's going to be one hell of a time." He gave her an impossibly beautiful smile and a wink, and then he was gone.

CHAPTER 4

Emma

"Vanity working on a weak head produces every sort of mischief."

- EMMA

Emma pulled her sporty red Kia straight into valet parking and sat for a moment, taking in the grandeur of the hotel entrance. She adjusted the car's rearview mirror down and applied a fresh coat of red lipstick to her plump lips. With one more satisfied glance in the mirror, she pulled her long blond locks to frame her face.

She exited the car, arranging her hat and sunglasses, and tossed the keys to the attendant as if staying at Mansfield was a common occurrence. Maybe her car didn't look like it belonged, but Emma made sure she did. She felt beautiful, confident, and, for once in her life, rich.

Oh, bless you, Fanny, for marrying a millionaire, she thought to herself. Stopping in front of the hotel entrance, she turned her phone to selfie mode and snapped a pic. She glanced down at the picture and frowned. She looked back at the lot, then rearranged herself to capture the shiny red BMW convertible with the personalized plate "LUXLIFE" in the frame. She snapped another picture and looked at it approvingly, her long, manicured nails flying over the keys. Her photo popped up instantly, captioned, *Mansfield Park, here I come! #MansfieldPark #Luxlife #Bertramwedding #fannnyandedmund #jealousmuch*

Emma felt both a rush of excitement and a pang of jealousy as she watched three women approach the valet. She took in every designer label she could see—Chanel, Hermès, Prada, Manolo Blahnik shoes, and Gucci glasses.

It took her a minute to realize she recognized two of them. "Julia! Mariah!" she exclaimed happily. Julia stopped short, squealed, and gave Emma a big hug.

Mariah pulled her sunglasses down and gave Emma an appraising glance.

"Oh my god, Emma! We just saw your sister, Anne. She hasn't changed a bit, but you...well, just look at you!" Julia said excitedly.

Emma made eye contact with the third woman and instantly recognized her from her book. Without waiting for the Bertrams to introduce her, she quickly reached out to shake her hand. "Caroline Bingley, a pleasure to meet you! I'm Emma Austen."

"Anne is your sister? Honey, bless her heart—it was almost impressive how effortlessly she could dishevel herself." Caroline gave Emma a limp handshake and a bored once-over. Then her eyes landed on Emma's Valentino Rockstud tote bag in bold red. "Love the bag, by the way. I have that one in green," she said with just a hint of admiration.

Emma flushed with pleasure. "Thanks, it's my favorite." It was also on loan from one of her many influencer friends. In fact, much of her wardrobe for the week ahead was on loan—a fact she would not be sharing with anyone, least of all Elinor, who, to Emma's annoyance, had been bugging her about getting a "real" job.

Julia quickly jumped in, "Well, listen, we are in a rush, but we will definitely have to catch up this week. We are just so thrilled y'all are here. Fanny will be tickled pink." She reached over and gave Emma a quick hug, and Mariah gave her a half-hearted wave goodbye.

Seeing the Bertram sisters brought back a flood of memories for Emma. The Bertram family had been a small piece of her childhood, but they had left a lasting impression on her. It was just so strange for Emma to think about how interconnected their lives were considering how differently they had grown up.

With four sisters, Emma's childhood had been chaotic, busy, and noisy, but Fanny was an only child. Their mothers were sisters, and the cousins had grown up near each other in the same small Kentucky town. Fanny had lost her mother first in a car accident, and then several years later, Emma and her sisters lost their own mother to cancer. The shared tragedies had forged a bond between the cousins that had lasted throughout their childhoods. But while the sisters grew up with very little, Fanny's father remarried a wealthy heiress, and Fanny had been whisked away to live in one of the most elite Kentucky neighborhoods. But he promised to keep the cousins close, so once a year, Emma and her sisters went out to spend the summer with Fanny. With its sprawling mansions, manicured gardens, and horse stables, Fanny's neighborhood was a far cry from the one in which the sisters shared two rooms in their modest brownstone.

It was during those summers that the sisters had first met the Bertrams, the wealthy family that lived on a neighboring estate to Fanny. The two Bertram daughters, Julia and Mariah, their brother Edmund, and his best friend George Knightley were often around when Emma and her sisters came to visit. Those summers were their first taste of life outside their small town, and Emma had been awed by the glamour and luxury of Fanny's life. It had been hard for her to accept how much Fanny had been given when she and her sisters had to work so hard for everything.

But Emma never forgot those summers, and she had fond memories of their time at Fanny's. As the cousins grew older, the visits had gradually stopped. And while the cousins had stayed in contact via occasional texts on birthdays and holidays, they had not been involved in one another's lives for many years now.

So it had come as a complete shock to hear that Fanny was marrying Edmund Bertram, and it was an even bigger surprise that she wanted her cousins to be her bridesmaids.

For Emma, this vacation was a dream come true. It was still hard for her to believe she was attending one of the biggest social events of the summer. The wedding was going to be a real who's who of the social and political scene. It offered her a huge opportunity to network with society's elite, and she planned to take full advantage of it. She'd been successful in growing her social media presence, and she'd gained a huge following. But, while being a brand ambassador for high-end designers had its perks, like lots of expensive clothes and freebies, it wasn't earning her the kind of money she wanted. She wanted the kind of money that could afford vacations at Mansfield.

Fanny's wedding was perfect timing. Emma had just launched her newest project, a dating app, and having Mansfield Resort as a sponsor and the engagement of clients with the Bertrams' wealth and status would be a huge boon.

She had eagerly reached out to Fanny to inquire about the esteemed guest list. She ticked off the names of the groomsmen: John Thorpe, Frank Churchill, John Willoughby, George Wickham, and William Elliot—all sons of politicians or wealthy businessmen, and, more importantly, all bachelors. Emma was already busy scheming about how she was going to get each of her bridesmaid sisters to post a "date" with the groomsmen at the resort.

For the first time, she really gave some thought to seeing her sisters. It had been at least two years since they were all together, since Elinor moved to Chicago. Her own move to Nashville had followed right after. She enjoyed the freedom that had come with moving away from her sisters, but she also missed them terribly.

She grinned, thinking of how she'd been able to talk her older sister, Elizabeth, into being her first "volunteer" to create a profile on her dating app. Although, judging from the ranting voicemail she received this morning, it sounded like her date had been an unmitigated disaster.

Emma chuckled to herself. She couldn't help but think that somehow, it was Elizabeth's fault. Elizabeth would never admit it, or maybe even recognize it, but she could be pretty intimidating. Emma didn't know many men who could handle her sister's blazing self-confidence and fiery self-assuredness. She could hardly wait to get all the juicy details when she saw her later today.

CHAPTER 5

Catherine

*"If adventures will not befall a young lady in her own
village, she must seek them abroad."*

- NORTHANGER ABBEY

At last, Catherine caught her first glimpse of Mansfield Park. She had finished her last exam of the semester that afternoon and was late in getting on the road. It was now just about sunset, but she made it!

The hotel itself looked imposing and made a foreboding silhouette against the dark red sky. Elongated windows and tall chimneys graced the horizon. It was still too light for the small, twinkling lights strung along the arbors and arches to be on, so the gardens had an eerie look in the last shadows of the day. The light mist moving in added to the ominous atmosphere around the resort.

Catherine laughed nervously to herself. Maybe listening to the *Southern Gothic* podcast on the drive up here hadn't been the best idea. Now her head was full of stories with vampires lurking in the dark and ghosts in the shadows. A sense of unease started to grow in her as she parked, the huge lot was deserted, not a soul in sight. She couldn't help but feel a sense of eeriness about the place, especially as the sun began to disappear.

What if she was kidnapped out here, no one would even know she was gone. Her heart beat a little faster and she palmed the small can of pepper spray she kept in her backpack. Her eyes vigilantly scanned the parking lot and she quickened her pace as she made her way toward the hotel entrance.

She felt an overwhelming sense of relief when she finally stepped into the lobby. Any hint of anxiety disappeared as she took in the room. Its crystal chandeliers were catching the last rays of the setting sun and sending light dancing around the walls. It was gorgeous, and it immediately took her breath away. She stood rooted in place, looking around in awe. A grand staircase occupied the center of the great hall. To the right was a sitting area, which had ornate chairs surrounding a huge marble fireplace. Twelve-foot windows opened onto a veranda that wrapped around the front of the hotel and looked out across the great lawn and gardens.

The grandeur and elegance of the place made her feel underdressed. Then she caught her reflection in a large golden-framed mirror, and her tattered jeans and tank top only made her feel more self-conscious. She pulled her hair out of its messy bun and let her strawberry-blond curls fall loosely over her shoulders. She straightened her posture, pulled her luggage toward her, and held tightly to a tattered copy of her favorite book.

She looked to her left and saw the registration desk. The young woman at the counter looked to be her own age, and her friendly smile immediately put Catherine at ease.

"Can I help you?" she heard the young woman ask. Catherine approached the counter and noticed the woman's name tag. Isabella.

"Yes, hi, I'm checking in. I'm Catherine Austen," she said timidly, setting her backpack and book on the counter.

Isabella glanced down at the novel, and her face lit up. "Oh, you're reading *Twilight*? That is my absolute favorite book—it's the reason I go by Bella. Isn't it just so romantic?" She sighed dreamily. Catherine smiled, taking an immediate liking to the girl.

To say she was a fan of the *Twilight* books would be an understatement. She had discovered the series as a teenager and became obsessed with Bella and Edward's story. Catherine wouldn't admit it to her sisters, but the thing she looked forward to most about this vacation wasn't the resort's grounds or amenities, but having the opportunity to curl up with her favorite book and just relax and read.

Shyly, Catherine said, "I can't even tell you how many times I've read it. I'm hoping to do another reread this week while I'm on vacation."

Bella took in Catherine's appearance and asked casually, "So, what brings you to Mansfield? I hope you don't take this the wrong way, but you don't look like most of the guests I check in. I mean, there's more Botox here than in Hollywood," she said in a hushed tone.

"I'm here for the Bertram wedding," said Catherine.

Bella gasped. "Oh, how lucky! I've been seeing all the preparations this week, and it looks like it's going to be such an amazing wedding. I'm jealous! I'd love to be invited to such an event," she said wistfully as she typed in Catherine's information.

Catherine took another look around the resort's lobby. "But you get to work here, surrounded by all of this every day—I'm jealous of you!"

Bella looked at Catherine skeptically but seemed to accept her sincerity. She looked around and then lowered her voice even more. "It's a beautiful place. If I just didn't have to deal with the people, it would be the perfect job." She sighed before continuing, "And, frankly, the Bertrams are the worst." She leaned conspiratorially across the counter. "Mrs. Bertram has a dog, and she insists we bring it room service. Room service for a dog! Can you imagine? I swear, what some people will do with their money just amazes me. She even named it Mrs. Norris, like it's a person!"

Catherine laughed. "Oh, I bet that's a Harry Potter reference. It's probably named after Filch's cat," she said amusingly.

Bella was not impressed. "Why would you name a dog after a cat? That's so stupid! The dog is so ugly; she should have named it after that big-eyed house elf. What was his name?"

"Dobby," said Catherine, a smile still on her face.

"Yes, that's the one! Anyway, we don't even allow pets. But of course, for people like the Bertrams, all kinds of exceptions are made." The resentment was clear in her voice. She went on: "Don't even get me started on Caroline Bingley! That woman is a terror. You would think she owns the place." Bella continued to ramble, "She practically demanded we ask all other guests to clear the pool area early in the morning, so she could have an undisturbed swim. I'm surprised she didn't ask for one of us to fan her with palm leaves while she lounges by the pool." Bella exaggeratedly rolled her eyes. And then, as if something just occurred to her, she gave a little gasp. "Oh god, I hope I haven't offended you! For all I know, you're related to them!" She looked horrified that she might have shared too much.

Catherine gave her an easy laugh in reassurance. "We aren't related to the Bertrams, but my cousin is the bride-to-be. So I guess, in a way, we'll be related soon. We knew the Bertrams when we were kids." Catherine thought about it. Could she even really say she knew the Bertrams? She had been so young when they'd visited Fanny. She had barely any recollection of Fanny's neighbors. However, Bella's mention of Mrs. Bertram's dog had struck a memory, and Catherine recalled how even back then, Edmund's mother never went anywhere without her beloved pug. She wondered if it was possible that it was the same dog after all these years.

Bella's face relaxed, but she resumed her professional manner. "Well, you're all set. It's showing that your sisters have arrived, and you will be sharing adjoining suites. Just head up the grand staircase and follow the signs for the garden-view rooms—Suites 204 and 205. Here is your room card, and we've also been asked to share the following itinerary with you, from your hosts." She handed Catherine an envelope. "This will tell you the planned activities for the week, rehearsal dinner information, and wedding details. I'm so jelly—you're going to have an amazing time!" She gave Catherine a longing smile. "I hope I see you again this week." Catherine thanked Bella and turned to make her way up the staircase.

From the landing, she looked over into the parlor and saw a woman sitting by the fireplace. There was a small pug nestled next to her on the couch. Catherine had no doubt she was Edmund's mother.

She thought of what Bella had told her, about room service for the dog, and giggled. Then she summoned her courage and walked over to introduce herself.

"Excuse me, Mrs. Bertram?" she asked shyly. The woman's eyes were closed; she appeared to be asleep. But hearing her name, she startled awake and caught Catherine's eye.

She continued timidly, "Mrs. Bertram, it's Catherine Austen. Do you remember me? I'm one of Fanny's cousins." She waited to see if the woman would show any sign of recognition.

Mrs. Bertram appeared a little confused, but she muttered, "Oh yes, my dear, delighted to see you."

Catherine continued, "I just wanted to personally thank you for your generosity this week and let you know how grateful my sisters and I are that you included us in the week's activities. It's so very kind of you."

Mrs. Bertram smiled absently. "Oh, all the plans this week are Julia and Mariah's doing. They are so good at this stuff. I know my dear Edmund would have been content to have a much smaller affair, but my daughters and husband would not hear of it. So, here we are." She sighed before adding, "It's such a strain on poor Mrs. Norris, you know. She gets very skittish outside of her normal routine."

But Mrs. Norris did not appear skittish or troubled as she lay snoring soundly next to Mrs. Bertram. Not even Catherine's interruption had roused the sleeping pup from her slumber.

Mrs. Bertram continued, "Neither one of us is in the best of health. It's such a trial when one is taken out of their daily comforts." Then Mrs. Bertram seemed to lose her place and again closed her eyes. Catherine tiptoed away and headed up the grand staircase.

She had just started up the stairs when she felt someone tug on her suitcase. She spun around to see a man who was still wearing his sunglasses in the lobby, his starched white shirt unbuttoned halfway down his chest. Catherine tried to look away from his hairy chest. A large gold Rolex, trousers that tapered at the ankle, and loafers with no socks completed his look.

"We can't have a pretty thing like you carrying her own suitcase," he said, and Catherine thought she caught a whiff of alcohol on his breath. Loosening her grip on the suitcase, she looked at him hesitantly. She was just about to thank him and assure him she could manage just fine when she realized he wasn't actually offering to carry it up himself.

"Hey, you!" he yelled, snapping his fingers at the young porter who had just entered the room. "I thought this place was rated five stars. Do you make all your guests carry their own luggage? Get on it, man."

Despite the berating, the young man kept his composure and hurried over to pick up Catherine's suitcase. "No problem, sir; I'll take care of it right now," the porter replied, a huge, friendly grin spreading across his face. "Here, let me help you, miss." He flashed Catherine his beautiful smile. She gave him a timid smile and a thank-you in return, handing him her room card and following him up the stairs.

"I can't believe how rude that man was to you. You shouldn't have to put up with that kind of treatment," she said, burning with indignation.

The porter appeared unfazed, but he surveyed her more closely. She felt his dark-gray eyes examine her. "Yeah, well, when your dad is on the most wanted list, I guess you can act like you own the place," he said, giving a little shrug.

Catherine's eyes went wide as she lowered her voice to say, "His dad is on the most wanted list? You mean he's wanted by the FBI!?"

He seemed confused, and then he burst out laughing, shaking his head. "No, not that list! Thorpe's dad is Senator Thorpe, from the finance committee. Everyone needs something from him, and people kiss up to him all the time. Thorpe's just throwing his weight around because his dad is a big shot, and because he can."

Catherine felt foolish for having misunderstood, and she blushed when she spoke. "Well, still. I'm sorry he treated you like that."

He stared at her again with his steady gaze, and she felt her pulse quicken. He gave a nod to the book still clutched tightly in her arm. "So, you're a reader," he said, grinning wide. "What book do you have there?"

Catherine glanced down at the worn pages of her copy of *Twilight* and blushed. It was one thing to admit to Bella how much she loved it, but she wasn't prepared to share that with this handsome stranger.

"*Twilight*," she replied hesitantly.

He sensed her embarrassment and said soothingly, "Don't worry, I'm a fan too. I've got a younger sister who convinced me to read it. It always makes me think of her now," he said, giving her his lopsided smile.

Catherine loved his easy manner and kindness. "You've actually read *Twilight?*" she said, beaming.

He continued to grin and said, "Well, don't give me too much credit. I only caved in and read it because my sister told me it had vampires. I wasn't expecting there to be romance." At that, Catherine let out a giggle. Then he added, "But I love to read, so I'll pretty much devour anything."

"Oh, me too," exclaimed Catherine. "I would be happy to spend my days doing nothing but reading." Just then, they arrived at her suite.

"Well, I hope you at least tear yourself away from your book long enough to enjoy the resort and your stay," he said politely. "I'm Henry, by the way. It's been a pleasure meeting you…"

"I'm Catherine," she said, feeling shy again.

"It was a pleasure, Catherine." He shook her hand, and a thrill went up her arm at his touch. "Henry Tilney, but can I let you in on a little secret?" He leaned in close to whisper in her ear, "I'm not actually the porter. I'm the assistant manager." With that, he gave a little smirk.

She looked at him wide eyed and flushed yet again with embarrassment. "Oh, I'm…I'm so sorry," she stammered. "Why didn't you say anything? You didn't have to help me."

His smile was mischievous. "Don't apologize. It gave me the chance to get to know you better. Besides, now you have something to write about in your journal tonight," he teased.

As he waved goodbye, she stood there, wondering how on Earth he could have known she kept a journal.

She inserted her key into Suite 204 and heard laughter coming from inside. The voices of her sisters made her realize how much she'd been looking forward to all of them being together. She entered cautiously and peeked in.

"Kitty Cat!" she heard as Emma opened the door all the way and immediately took Catherine into a warm embrace, effortlessly balancing a champagne flute in one hand.

CHAPTER 6

Elinor

"Do not let the behavior of others destroy your inner peace."

- SENSE AND SENSIBILITY

Elinor took in the sight of her four sisters and beamed with happiness. All together at last. In just two short years, she saw perceptible changes in her younger siblings.

She watched as Emma handed Catherine a flute of champagne and was on the verge of saying something when she remembered her youngest sister turned twenty-one this past year.

Elizabeth, always a force to be reckoned with, now carried herself with the confidence of a poised businesswoman.

The changes in Emma were the most surprising to Elinor. From her wardrobe to her attitude, she exuded an air of sophistication that only heightened her own feelings of frumpiness.

Anne, always steady and reliable, was the only one of her sisters who seemed unchanged.

Watching them all, she felt a mix of pride, nostalgia

and the bittersweet realization, that while some things had stayed the same, so much had changed.

Emma pulled her sisters close and drew out her phone. "Now that we are all together, we need a selfie! C'mon, crowd in and hold up your glasses!"

Elinor groaned, "Really, Em? I haven't had a chance to freshen up. This isn't going on Facebook!"

Emma gave a reproachful glance. "You do know that no one's on Facebook anymore, right? I swear, Elli, you're such an old lady." Emma's retorts always had a way of getting to the heart of Elinor's insecurities. But Emma continued, oblivious to having inflicted any slights.

"Cat, you're in here with me and Anne! Elli and Lizzy are next door. You have to come check out the view from our balcony—we have an amazing view of the gardens! We had champagne waiting for us, and a platter of chocolate-covered strawberries!" Emma rambled on, hardly containing her enthusiasm.

Catherine laughed, "This hotel is so fancy! I felt out of place just walking around the lobby."

Emma's steely blue eyes looked pointedly at her sister. "Fitting in is about attitude, not clothes, Cat. Just act like you belong, and fake it till you make it," she said, taking another swig of champagne.

Elinor took in Emma's beautifully tailored look. "Easy for you to say, Em! You're wearing Gucci and Johnny Choo shoes, looking like you stepped off the cover of a magazine," Elinor grumbled, trying not to sound bitter.

"First of all, it's Prada, and second of all, they are *Jimmy* Choo shoes," Emma replied, but without any hint of offense. "Just one of the perks of the job," she said proudly.

"You don't have a job." Elinor winced at how quickly the retort had popped out of her mouth, and she instantly regretted it when she saw a flash of hurt cross her sister's face.

Emma sighed. "I don't think you realize how much work goes into what I do, Elinor. But nothing is going to spoil my good mood. Look at this place; it's amazing!" Anne quickly chimed in, "You used to love to dress up, Elli. Don't you remember when we'd play *Little Women* and you always wanted to be Meg so you could wear Mom's heels?"

Elinor immediately softened and smiled at the memory. "I had forgotten all about that," she said, nostalgia sweeping over her. "Mom would have loved this for Fanny, and she'd be so happy we are all together."

"You guys always made me play the tragic role of Beth even though I wanted to be Jo," Anne continued, her smile barely concealed by her pretend scowl.

"Yeah, how come Lizzy always got to be Jo?" Emma asked, laughing now.

Catherine chimed in, "I don't know what you're complaining about, Em! At least you got to be Amy. All the March sisters were taken, so I always had to be Laurie. It took me a while to figure out he was a boy."

At that, they all burst out laughing.

"Well, we're all going to have the chance to dress up this week—I can't believe we have designer bridesmaid dresses. I can hardly wait to see what Fanny chose for us," Emma said excitedly.

Elizabeth groaned. "We don't even know what the dresses look like. What if they're those horrible frilly ones with ruffles or bows?"

Anne smiled. "I don't think I've ever seen you in a dress, Lizzy. I can't wait to see you all dolled up!" she teased, and Elizabeth looked miserable at the thought.

"Honestly, I don't know why you're all worried about fitting in here. All of these people are so fake. Did you see how much plastic surgery these women have? I just don't understand this shallow obsession with appearances.

Sorry, but nothing about that lifestyle appeals to me," Elizabeth said with conviction.

Emma was incredulous. "Look around, Lizzy. This right here…this is the life, and we only get to experience it for one week. I don't know about you all, but I intend to enjoy every minute of it," she said, taking another swig of champagne.

Anne jumped in, again trying to keep the peace. "Speaking of obsessed with their appearance, guess who I ran into? Julia and Mariah! How long has it been since we've seen them? I swear, they are just as mean now as they were back then."

Emma said, "I ran into them too! I thought they looked fabulous. I would kill for Mariah's Chanel dress! And Julia's shoes!" She gave a wistful sigh.

Elizabeth narrowed her eyes at her sister. "That's my whole point. Who cares what they were wearing? They're snobs. Julia and Mariah were never nice to us when we were kids. They went out of their way to make us feel like we didn't belong. The only one they even tolerated was you, Em. I can just imagine how much worse they are as adults," she said indignantly.

"Oh, and I almost forgot," Anne interjected excitedly, "I met Caroline Bingley! You know the model from that famous cover of Vogue? She's even more beautiful in person."

"Is she the one who just published her memoir? I think it's called *The Accomplished Woman*." Elinor asked curiously. Caroline's memoir was everywhere, and she had recently considered buying a copy.

Elizabeth rolled her eyes. "I just don't get why her book is so popular. Who is buying that crap? I'm sorry, but what makes her so "accomplished" just because she was born rich?"

Emma considered her sister's words. "Did it ever occur to you, Lizzy, that maybe you were the one who was a snob? You never even tried to fit in with Julia and Mariah; you made up your mind not to like them from the start. And I happen to have bought Caroline's book—she's a successful businesswoman and has lots of great advice. If you weren't so quick to judge, you might actually like it too."

Elizabeth sighed. "I'm just saying, I'm not sure we should be happy for Fanny. I'm sad to think that this is the kind of family she's marrying into, that these are the people she will be surrounded by," she said. "I'm having a hard time even picturing Fanny with snobs like the Bertrams."

"I wouldn't waste your time feeling sorry for Fanny. She's going to be rich beyond our wildest dreams, and more power to her," Emma said, raising her glass and finishing off the last drop of yet another glass of champagne.

"Maybe you should slow down on the drinks, Em," Elinor heard herself say, which again she regretted immediately. Why did she have this compulsive need to comment on her sisters' choices? She was getting on her own nerves.

Emma appeared not to take offense. She walked over to the bottle, poured another glass, and handed it to Elinor. "Elli, you just need to chill. We don't need a mom this week."

Elinor reluctantly took the glass. Emma was right, she needed to let herself relax.

"I still can't believe the Bertrams' generosity, paying for our stay here." Catherine marveled.

"And it's not just the hotel rooms that are paid for," Emma exclaimed gleefully. "Fanny didn't want us worrying about anything this week. *Everything* is covered. We just need to charge it to the room. I plan to enjoy every freebie and luxury available."

"So, has anyone seen Fanny yet?" Anne asked, happily

DEE BLANKENSHIP

dipping a strawberry into her glass of champagne.

Catherine chimed in, "No, but I did see Mrs. Bertram on my way up here, and I don't think she has changed at all. Wasn't she always kind of out of it?"

Elizabeth scoffed, "She must still be popping too many pills! And she always had that horrid little mutt."

"Yes! The little monster was sitting with her down in the parlor," Catherine said with a giggle. "I only remember meeting her a few times, but she seemed the same."

Anne responded, "I hardly remember her at all, but I do remember the dog."

"Really?" Emma said, surprised. "I remember everything about those summers. They are some of my favorite memories."

Elizabeth caught Emma's eye with a knowing look. "That's because you had a crush on Edmund's best friend even though he was way older than you," Elizabeth said. "You followed that poor boy around like a puppy dog."

"Oh wow, I remember that! You were always trying to tag along with George," Elinor said. She had a sudden memory of Edmund's best friend, George Knightley. He had been closer to her own age than Emma's, but that hadn't stopped Emma from having a huge crush on him. She let her mind drift back, she had her own fond memories of those carefree summers.

"Really, you think I had a crush on George?" Emma scoffed. "I just wanted to do what the boys were doing." She quickly changed the subject.

"Come look at the week's itinerary," she said as she unclasped a large envelope and pulled out a sheet of embossed paper. "This week is going to be truly amazing!" she marveled while laying it on the bed for all to see. Elinor was shaking her head in wonder, "I still can't believe this is all paid for!"

Emma giggled and declared, "And I, for one, am taking full advantage of their generosity!"

46

A knock at the door interrupted their reunion. Emma jumped up first. "Oh, I bet that's the room service I ordered!"

Elinor frowned. "Room service? Do you know how much that costs at a place like this?"

Emma paused on her way to the door and gave her sister a scowl. "You just got through saying it's all paid for, Elinor. What's the problem?"

Elinor was asking herself the same question. But she had already been feeling uncomfortable about the Bertrams footing the bill for their stay, and seeing Emma's eagerness to rack up charges only heightened her concern.

Emma yanked the door open, but instead of finding room service, Fanny was standing there.

Emma let out a delighted squeal and pulled her cousin into a big hug. "Fanny! Love, we were just talking about you!"

The sisters quickly joined in, wrapping their cousin in warm embraces. As Elinor stepped back, she took in her cousin's striking appearance. Always petite, Fanny seemed even smaller beside them now, her delicate features framed by cascades of dark curls.

There was an understated grace about her, nothing flashy or ostentatious. She wore a simple yet polished outfit of black jeans, a crisp white blouse, and heels that still left her several inches shorter than her cousins. The only jewelry she wore was a silver cross on a chain around her neck and an engagement ring with a small solitaire diamond. Elinor was struck by how Fanny's poise and simple elegance made her fit right in at Mansfield.

Fanny beamed at her cousins. "I can't believe you're all here! You don't know how happy I am to see you. We have so much planned, and it just means a lot to me that you all came." At this, she got a little teary-eyed.

Elinor reached over and gave Fanny another hug. "What can we do for you this week? We would love to help in any way we can."

Fanny gave her a grateful smile. "Absolutely nothing. Everything is covered! We have a wedding planner, and of course Julia and Mariah are taking care of some smaller details. I just want y'all to relax and have fun! Mansfield is an amazing place." Fanny was positively glowing with happiness.

Still, Elinor couldn't shake the uneasy feeling as she watched her cousin, radiant with excitement, talk about her upcoming wedding. She worried that Fanny was caught up in the fairytale and had no idea how to navigate the expectations and scrutiny that would come with marrying into such wealth.

There was another loud knocking at the door. "Now *that* will be room service!" Emma exclaimed smiling.

Bertram Wedding Itinerary

Wednesday June 11th
Golfing on the Greens ~ The golf course will be exclusively for wedding party guests from 8:00am–12:00noon
The Mansfield Spa ~ Spa treatments, manicures, facials, and massages available from 8:00am – 5:00pm.
Cocktail Hour ~ bride and groom arrive, cocktails and hors d'oeuvres from 7:00pm – 8:30pm.

Thursday June 12th
A Day at the Races ~ The hotel will provide a limousine shuttle service to Northcumberland Park Racetrack for wedding guests attending the Cumberland Stakes.

Friday June 13th
Rehearsal ~ Wedding party gather at Mansfield Gardens at 4:00pm.
Dinner reception begins at 5:30pm.

Saturday June 14th
Wedding Ceremony ~
Please join us at the Mansfield Gardens Pavilion for the wedding of Fanny Price and Edmund Bertram.
4:00pm sharp.
Reception to immediately follow

CHAPTER 7

Elizabeth

"Angry people are not always wise."

- PRIDE AND PREJUDICE

Elizabeth awoke early the next morning. She knew her sisters well enough to know that it would be at least an hour before anyone else was up. It had been a late night catching up and plenty of champagne had been consumed.

She tiptoed out onto the balcony to avoid awakening Elinor. Their room had a stunning view of the garden's luscious greenery and beautifully cultivated flowers. She glanced down at the time on her phone—plenty of time to take a run around the gardens and enjoy the crisp morning air.

She pulled on her sweatpants, threw her hair into a ponytail, and made her way down to the grounds. Her mood soared as she walked along the veranda and down toward the garden.

It was going to be a beautiful day. The sun was already shining, but the oppressive heat was still at bay. Elizabeth enjoyed a light jog past fountains, statues, and topiaries, marveling at the care that went into the resort's upkeep.

This jog was a good opportunity to clear her head.

Last night's conversation with Emma had consumed her thoughts. She hadn't realized how much she missed her sisters until they were all together. It was so easy to fall back into their usual banter and laughter, but reuniting reminded her how very different they all were.

She understood Emma the least. Her sister's need for approval from people Elizabeth saw as shallow and pretentious was something she could not understand. She didn't share Emma's desire to impress. While she loved the resort's beauty, it was tiresome to be around people who cared so much about expensive cars, designer jewelry, and brand labels.

What do these people know about life's real problems? she mused to herself.

She stopped to catch her breath and looked out across the grounds. A large white tent adorned with a canopy of fairy lights caught her eye and she realized that this was probably the spot for Fanny's reception.

She wandered along the path to get a closer look. From inside the tent, there was a fantastic view of the man-made lake. She had to admit, this really was a fairytale location.

Startled out of her thoughts by a woman's voice behind her, she turned to see a couple standing near one of the benches that looked out over the lake.

"Excuse me, miss? This is private property," the haughty woman said in a strong southern accent.

Elizabeth took in the woman's appearance. She was tall, much taller than Elizabeth. She wore a gorgeous floral wrap dress, a silk scarf around her neck, and oversized Gucci sunglasses. She would have been incredibly beautiful if it weren't for the sour look on her face—a look that was aimed straight at Elizabeth.

"Honey, these gardens are for guests of the resort only. They aren't open to the public," she said, eyeing Elizabeth coldly.

Elizabeth felt her indignation rise and started to respond, but she was startled when the man spoke her name.

"Elizabeth?"

She caught her breath as she realized she was looking straight into the gaze of Darcy Fitzwilliam. Darcy, of the infamous disastrous date. The man who told her she was not 'his type', the man she hoped to never run into again—like, ever—was here, standing in front of her, at Mansfield. Her mind raced as she tried to figure out how this could be.

"Darcy?" was the only word she could muster.

"Are you stalking me?" he asked coolly, and Elizabeth was about to laugh when she realized by his grave expression that it was a genuine question.

"Am I stalking you? Are you serious right now? Good god, of course I'm not stalking you! What kind of question is that!?" She was so flustered she couldn't think straight.

"Well then, what are you doing here at Mansfield?" he demanded.

Elizabeth drew herself up a little straighter. "I'm…I'm a guest here," she replied, sounding more unsure of herself than she was hoping to.

"You're a guest here? At Mansfield?" Darcy replied, a little incredulous.

Her anger bolstered her confidence. "Is that so hard to believe?" she asked, her voice filled with fury.

She heard the woman mutter, "Frankly, yes."

Darcy turned to the woman and then back to Elizabeth. "Elizabeth, this is Caroline Bingley. Caroline, this is Elizabeth Austen."

Recognition dawned on her. This was the woman

Anne and Emma had been discussing yesterday. The model with the memoir.

Caroline rolled her eyes. "Good lord, just how many of you are there?"

"How many of us are there?" Elizabeth repeated, puzzled. She was still trying to get her bearings that Darcy was here at Mansfield.

"Yes, I've already met two of your sisters, and I'm just curious how many more of you I should be prepared to meet," Caroline said, glancing down at her beautifully manicured nails as if bored by the conversation.

Elizabeth, refusing to be intimidated, responded cordially, "I'm here with my four sisters." She looked back at Darcy. "Our cousin is getting married," she added by way of explanation.

"Oh, that's right. I remember Mariah saying that her father was paying for Fanny's family to stay here this week. How lucky for you all," Caroline said. When her eyes swept over Elizabeth, there was an insincere smile on her face.

Elizabeth refused to give Caroline the satisfaction of knowing how much her comment bothered her, especially in front of Darcy. She responded with as much enthusiasm as she could muster, "Yes, the Bertrams have been very generous to us."

Caroline turned to leave. "Let's go Darcy, I've got a nail appointment at the spa to get to." Elizabeth's eyes flickered again to Caroline's already perfectly manicured nails.

She was surprised when Darcy responded, "Go on without me, Caroline. I'll be right behind you."

Clearly annoyed, Caroline turned and walked away without giving Elizabeth another glance.

"Well, she seems nice," Elizabeth said, rolling her eyes and making no attempt to hide her sarcasm.

Darcy studied her for a moment, and when he spoke he

sounded a little contrite. "I apologize for my assumption; I was just surprised to see you here."

"Oh, so you don't make it a practice to accuse women of following you around?" She couldn't help her urge to increase his discomfort.

He said nothing, but his deepening embarrassment deflated Elizabeth's anger, and she looked at him inquisitively. "So, I take it you are here for the wedding as well? How do you know the Bertrams?" *Of course he knows the Bertrams*, she thought. *Everyone with money knows the Bertrams.*

Darcy met her gaze. Here outside, in the sunshine, his eyes were more golden brown than they had seemed in the poorly lit restaurant. She suddenly remembered what she looked like, sweaty from her run, and inwardly groaned.

Why was she always a total disaster when she ran into this man?

He continued to hold her gaze as he answered, "My aunt is actually very close to Edmund's mother. Caroline is friends with Edmund's sisters."

"Are you two dating?" Now she flushed with embarrassment, mad at her own impulsiveness. What on Earth had possessed her to ask that?

But once again, Darcy appeared more embarrassed than she did. "No. No, we aren't dating. I wouldn't have gone on a date with you if I were dating someone else," he said, a little indignantly.

Suddenly, a thought occurred to Elizabeth. "Did Edmund ask you to sign up for the dating app?"

Darcy gave a little smile. It was the first time she had seen him with anything other than a scowl on his face, and she didn't want to admit that it made him even more handsome. He answered softly, "Edmund mentioned that Fanny was trying to help out her cousin with a new venture. He asked a few of us to 'volunteer' to sign up.

I picked that obscure library restaurant thinking no one else would find it interesting, but..." He let a little chuckle escape. "Obviously I was wrong."

"Not something you're used to apparently," Elizabeth said, unable to be civil for some reason.

Darcy continued, "That was my first time using a dating app. I can assure you, based on the disastrous results, it isn't something I'll be doing again."

Elizabeth tried to decide if she should feel insulted that Darcy thought their date was "disastrous" or flattered that he had opted to meet her in the first place.

As if he suddenly remembered he needed to be somewhere, he said, "Well, I won't hold you up any longer, Elizabeth. I assume I'll be seeing more of you this week." Then he gave her a little nod and walked off hurriedly.

Not if I see you first, she thought to herself. But as she headed back up along the path, she couldn't help smiling.

***

By the time she'd returned to the resort and freshened up, she found her sisters had all made it down to breakfast and were seated on the outside veranda, ordering up mimosas.

"Don't look now, Lizzy," Emma started, "but we are checking out the, um, scenery at the far table."

Elizabeth scooted her chair a little sideways and picked up a menu. She peeked over it in what she hoped was a nonchalant manner. There were four men seated around the table, their boisterous laughter and loud conversation ringing out across the patio. Elizabeth had to admit they were a handsome looking group. They seemed to be having a good time...with the exception of one, who appeared to be suffering from what she guessed was a hangover.

Catherine piped up, "That guy hugging his Bloody Mary is a real douchebag!"

Emma laughed. "You never say anything mean about anyone, Cat! What did he do to you?"

"He's just loud and rude, and he treats the people who work here like crap," Catherine said, an uncommon frown coming over her face.

"Uh-huh, and who do you know who works here, Cat?" Emma pried, looking teasingly at her younger sister.

Catherine blushed and said, "Well, only the porter who carried up my bags." Then she quickly interjected, "Oh, but it turned out he wasn't the porter after all."

They each glanced at her, waiting for further explanation, but Catherine began sipping her mimosa, oblivious to their curious stares and confusion.

"Is it just me, or does one of them look like Prince William?" Emma giggled.

Elizabeth looked over and thought that was a pretty accurate description. He was tall, with blondish-brown hair that lopped over to one side and blue eyes. He caught Elizabeth's eye and gave her a wolfish smile.

Great, not only was she caught ogling him, but now she could feel her cheeks heat up with a flush.

He remained seated, but two of his friends rose up and walked toward their table.

"Don't look now, but Mr. Cowboy and Captain America are heading our way," Emma giggled, sipping her mimosa and peering out over her large sunglasses.

Anne glanced over. "Oh, I actually know one of them already! Mr. Cowboy is one of Edmund's groomsmen. His name is John Willoughby, or, as his friends call him"— and here Anne went into a perfect Texas drawl—"Jay Doubleya." They were all laughing as the men sauntered up.

"Well, looks like this is the party table," Mr. Cowboy

said as he leaned down and glanced around the table. "Good morning, ladies! I'm JW, and this here is my friend Frank Churchill."

This introduction caused all the sisters to enter into fits of laughter once again, for Anne had expertly captured his Southern drawl.

Undeterred, he continued, "Me and my buddy are looking to put together a foursome." His grin spread across his entire face. "For golf, of course," he said with a wink.

With an easy grin, Frank Churchill spoke up. "One of our buddies isn't feeling his best this morning, so we were hoping to charm one of you lovely ladies into joining us." His bright eyes and dazzling smile landed directly on Emma, who removed her sunglasses and took a long sip of her drink. Elizabeth admired her sister's cool, casual demeanor.

Then Emma looked back up at him and practically cooed her regrets. "Well, Frank, that's just a darn shame, because we already have plans for the day. But you boys have fun chasing balls." She gave him her biggest, sweetest smile.

"I'll join you," Elizabeth heard herself say.

Frank looked visibly disappointed, but JW let out a whoop and said, "Well, alright, that's what I'm talking about! How about we meet you down at the clubhouse in an hour?"

After the men walked off, Anne turned to tease Elizabeth. Still laughing, she asked, "Lizzy, do you even play golf, or are you just interested in getting to know them a little better? I have to say, I wouldn't peg them as your type. Isn't that what they usually call a rake in those romance novels you love so much?"

"Yeah," Elinor agreed, "I totally pegged you as the sunshine-and-grump duo type. These two seem a little too cheerful for your taste."

"Well, I'm glad I've amused you all." Elizabeth tried to sound indignant but was unable to hide the laughter in her voice. "I hate to disappoint you, but I have zero interest in Mr. Texas or his friend. I'll have you all know, I'm actually quite good at golf," she said smugly. Her sisters looked at her curiously, which made her continue, "Do y'all know how many book deals get cut on the golf course? I needed an in." She shrugged. "So I took golf lessons," she pronounced with a satisfied grin.

Catherine looked up at her sister in admiration. "You really are fierce, Lizzy."

"Cheers to that," said Emma, and held up her glass for a toast.

CHAPTER 8

Elinor

"If I could but know his heart, everything would become easy."

-SENSE AND SENSIBILITY

E linor remained seated at the breakfast table for a while after her sisters left. Elizabeth returned to the room to get ready to hit the golf course, while Anne, Emma, and Catherine headed down to the spa. They had tried to persuade Elinor to join them, but she insisted she had a few hours of work to do and would catch up with them later. She'd planned to head back to the room but got distracted watching, with amusement, the group of young men across the patio.

The two gentlemen who'd approached the sisters about golf had returned to their friends, and a few more had joined them. Elinor marveled at their confidence and charisma. The group exuded an undeniable magnetism, and she found herself watching them unabashedly.

She was startled out of her spying by a woman's high-pitched voice. "Do you mind if I join you?"

Elinor looked up to find a distinguished older woman, somewhere near her sixties, pulling out a chair and taking a seat. Obviously, the woman was not anticipating Elinor would say no. She smiled brightly and added, "It's just that you looked like you could use a companion, and my friends haven't come down to breakfast yet. I thought maybe you wouldn't mind a little company."

Elinor would not dream of saying no, so she leaned over and introduced herself. "That would be lovely. I'm Elinor Austen; so pleased to meet you," she said, giving the woman a gracious smile.

"I'm Mrs. Jennings. I come to Mansfield every summer. Although I must say, it's very exciting this year—what with the Bertram wedding and all its distinguished guests." She paused for a moment as she looked at Elinor, before continuing, "I know the Bertrams personally and was quite honored to be included on the guest list. Although I'm sure it's just because this is the week I'm always here, but still it's delightful to be included." Then she nudged Elinor teasingly. "I saw you watching those handsome gentlemen over there."

The abrupt change in subject caught Elinor by surprise, and she felt a warm rush to her cheeks. "You've embarrassed me, Mrs. Jennings. I was only entertained by their antics." She felt she had to explain herself. The thought of Mrs. Jennings believing she had any interest in the men was mortifying to her.

She changed the subject back to the wedding. "I'm actually here for the wedding too. My sisters and I are the bride's cousins; we are going to be her bridesmaids."

But Mrs. Jennings was not to be diverted from her favorite topic, and Elinor's attempt only gave her more steam. "Well, then you must know that your young men friends over there are the groomsmen. It's quite a distinguished group." She glanced back over to the men, who were now all standing. She leaned conspiratorially close to Elinor and said, "Shall I fill you in?"

Elinor could not help but be amused by her eagerness as she found herself leaning in closer to hear.

Mrs. Jennings began, "Now, the gentleman with the cowboy boots, and dare I say the most handsome of the group—but then, as a younger woman I was always partial to a man in the saddle—that's John Willoughby. His father is one of the most politically powerful businessmen in Texas. Made his money in oil and natural gas." She lowered her voice and leaned in even closer to Elinor. "Rumor has it, though, that he's cut his son off, won't give him another dime. Not a single penny. Seems JW has a problem with-," she put her hand up to her mouth, spelling out slowly, "-D-I-C-E," shaking her head in disapproval.

Elinor tried to suppress a giggle, not sure why Mrs. Jennings felt the need to spell it out. "You mean he likes to gamble?" asked Elinor, taking guilty pleasure in listening to the woman's colorful commentary.

Mrs. Jennings nodded. "Let's just say Lady Luck has not been on his side." Then she continued, "Now, the one with the sexy British accent and the mischievous grin—he was the groom's roommate at Oxford. His name is George Wickham. His father is a duke! No, that's not right…he's an earl. Or, wait, is it a magistrate?" She stopped, momentarily lost in her thoughts. "Well, one of those, anyway."

Elinor looked closely at the young man. He was the one Emma had likened to Prince William, and he did look like the young prince…at least before he lost all his hair. She couldn't help thinking that in a few years, Wickham would look even more like William, as his hair already showed signs of receding.

"Let's see, the one that looks like a football quarterback, that's John Thorpe. A nasty young man," Mrs. Jennings said with a look of distaste. "It's no secret he is a little too fond of the D-R-I-N-K." Again, she slowly spelled out the word to Elinor's amusement. "His father is a senator and, well, let's just say...like father, like son," she said, making a tsk-tsk noise.

Mrs. Jennings went on, "Now, that smoldering hunk with the dark skin and light eyes is Will Elliot." Elinor gave a gasp of surprise at the older woman's bold description.

Mrs. Jennings cackled. "Honey, I may be old, but I can still look," she said, and her eyes lingered on the handsome Mr. Elliot, much to Elinor's discomfort. "Now, there's a story there!" She leaned in even closer to Elinor. "Let's just say his mother wasn't Mrs. Elliot! Seems his father had an affair with the help." She rolled her eyes in exasperation. "A tale as old as time. Anyway, his uncle owns the renowned Kellynch Farms, a horse farm not far from here. He won't have anything to do with his nephew, though. Doesn't approve of his brother's illegitimate son. I think Will's got a chip on his shoulder because of it. But he's done well for himself without his uncle's money," she said approvingly.

Elinor knew she shouldn't encourage Mrs. Jennings, but she was curious about the other gentleman who had approached their table earlier, the one who was so obviously interested in Emma. "What do you know about the sandy haired one? The one who's a little more..." Elinor's voice drifted as she searched for the word.

"Built? Is that the word you're looking for?" Mrs. Jennings let out a rambunctious laugh. "Yes, I see your type now," she said, wagging a finger at Elinor, who blushed. "That's Frank Churchill. He wasn't born into money, but he was raised in it. Yep, that boy was lucky, alright. Adopted by one of the wealthiest families in the state. But, yes—I think 'built' is a good word for that one." She gave Elinor a huge grin. "Is he the one you had your eye on?" she said, looking expectantly at Elinor.

"I'm sorry to disappoint you, Mrs. Jennings," Elinor said with a shy smile, "but I already have someone back home." She felt a little guilty about her white lie, but Mrs. Jennings just gave her a knowing smile.

"Oh, to be twenty years younger," Mrs. Jennings sighed.

Elinor tried to suppress a smile. She was pretty sure it was closer to forty years younger, but she gave the older woman a polite nod.

Mrs. Jennings smiled warmly in return. "Well, dear, I've enjoyed our little chat, but my friends have arrived for breakfast. I do hope you enjoy your stay. Mansfield is definitely magical." She gave Elinor a little wink and walked off.

***

Elinor returned to the suite. She pulled out her sketch pad and plopped down into the large chaise lounge that looked out across the famed Mansfield Gardens. A stab of guilt coursed through her for having chosen to return to the room rather than spend the day with her sisters.

It was just that her thoughts felt so jumbled right now, and she longed for a little peace and quiet. When her mind was this occupied, it always did her good to draw.

She busily set about sketching, and her mind wandered to Eddie. When had he started to occupy so many of her thoughts?

Elinor had collaborated with several authors over the past two years. Her focus was always on the work. In fact, she rarely spent much time with her clients other than to get their vision for the story and discuss initial ideas.

But something had been different with Eddie from the start. Normally reserved and shy, he seemed to come alive when sharing stories from his childhood. Elinor noticed how his usual quiet demeanor transformed into excitement and animation as he spoke. That same passion flowed into his writing, captivating her. She especially loved his vivid stories of growing up in India.

Bringing his stories to life was easy for her and she had never been more excited about a project. Her whimsical sketches were some of her best work, and Eddie loved all her ideas.

Over time, their conversations took on a life beyond work-related matters, drifting into discussions about their favorite books, family dynamics and career aspirations.

Eddie shared that his parents had emigrated from India when he was a young teen, but they held tight to their cultural traditions. They had high expectations for their eldest son. Expected to follow in his father's footsteps by entering the medical field and becoming a doctor; he had let them down when he dropped out of medical school to follow his dream of becoming a writer.

Elinor could see the hurt and confusion in Eddie's eyes when he talked about disappointing his family. It was unfathomable to her that any parent could be disappointed in a son who had Eddie's kind nature and talent, and her heart ached to see him hurting.

Over time, Elinor realized her feelings for him might be evolving into something more than friendship. She increasingly looked forward to time spent together and she suspected that Eddie might have similar feelings.

But any hope Elinor had clung to faded when Eddie confided to her that his parents expected him to marry someone of their choosing. He explained that arranged marriages were common in India, especially for the eldest son. His parents wanted him to marry Lakshmi, a young woman he had known since they were both children.

The declaration was a bittersweet revelation to Elinor. She knew he was conflicted over his feelings, yet he had disappointed his family once and would not do it again.

She had taken the news stoically, never letting her true feelings show, never giving any hint to the turmoil she was feeling inside. She resigned herself to the fact that they would just remain good friends.

But that didn't mean she had given up all hope. In moments of weakness, she often found herself scrolling through Lakshmi's social media. It felt wrong but she couldn't help herself.

Lakshmi went by Lucy and seemed to have a prolific online presence and a busy social life. From her frequent posts, it was obvious that she enjoyed clubbing and partying with her friends. *Not at all Eddie's type,* Elinor thought. It was also interesting that there wasn't a single photo of Lucy and Eddie together.

She convinced herself it was ok to hope.

Setting her sketchbook aside, she turned her attention to her laptop. Although she could pretend she was simply logging on to check her emails, deep down she knew the real reason – she hoped to see if Eddie was online. She hated how much she missed him.

As soon as the screen lit up, a notification from Eddie appeared, grabbing her attention instantly.

This is NOT what one does on vacation! Why are you working?

She smiled to herself, typing in reply, *My options today were golfing with the female version of Tiger Woods or hanging out in the spa with Audrey Hepburn. I don't think my ego could take either. Lol.*

Don't do that, he typed back. *Don't compare yourself so unfairly to your sisters. You're the most talented woman I know.*

Elinor felt a hot flush sweep across her face, a warmth of feeling.

Speaking of your sisters, how is everyone getting along? You're not being too bossy are you? He added a smiley face emoji.

She loved that, as the oldest child in his family, he, too,

understood how the responsibility of the younger siblings rested on their shoulders.

She responded with a grimacing emoji.

He typed back, *LOL! Well, at least you tried. So, tell me about Mansfield. You know I'm jealous that you are in the lap of luxury.*

She described the resort in vivid detail, painting a picture of it's breathtaking scenery.

Elinor, that sounds amazing. I wish I could see it for myself.

Her fingers hovered over the keyboard as she typed, *I wish that too,* but before she could send it, she hesitated and erased the words. This was their unspoken dance, always skirting the edge, never daring to step over the line.

Instead, she replied, *I'm sure you would spend all your time exploring the topiary garden.*

WHAT!! There are topiaries?! You never told me that. How are you not down there right now, taking a leisurely stroll through the masterpieces?

Elinor chuckled. One of Eddie's books had been a journey to the Hanging Gardens of Mumbai, and she had spent hours sketching the sculpted animals it described.

I knew that would make you jealous, she typed. Then she added, *Not everyone shares your love of topiaries, Eddie, but I promise I'll send some pics.*

He sent a laughing emoji and typed, *I've got to go now. Make sure you have fun, Elli. And let's talk when you get back?*

She paused before replying, *Sounds good, Eddie. Take care.*

Let's talk? About what?! And it didn't escape her notice that this was the first time he'd ever called her Elli. She closed her laptop, smiling dreamily.

CHAPTER 9

Elizabeth

"You were disgusted with the women who were always speaking and looking, and thinking for your approbation alone. I roused, and interested you, because I was so unlike them."

- PRIDE AND PREJUDICE

Elizabeth made her way down to the fairway. It was early morning, and the air felt fresh. There was still a coat of dew on the grass. Little pockets of fog were fading across the grounds. This is what she loved about golf. The chance to be outdoors, enjoy nature, and get exercise. Plus, it was a game that challenged her both mentally and physically.

She was pleased with herself for keeping her own set of golf clubs in the back of her car. She hadn't planned on golfing at Mansfield Park because she knew none of her sisters would be interested, but she had brought them anyway. The offer to get out on a course was one she couldn't resist, even if it meant spending the morning with JW and his friends. She knew her sisters would be amused and tease her that she was only going for the company, but now that she was out here, she was actually looking forward to getting in a little practice.

She walked around to the starter window to see if JW was there, vaguely curious who would be joining them. She saw JW standing not with Frank Churchill, as she'd expected, but with the gentleman she had embarrassingly made eye contact with at breakfast. As she approached, he gave her an easy smile and a wave. Then he leaned over and held out his hand to shake hers.

"Hello. George Wickham, but my friends call me Wick. You must be Elizabeth." When he spoke, he had the most gorgeous British accent.

Elizabeth found herself staring a little too long and blushing for the second time that morning. "I'm glad you boys had an opening. I was hoping to get in a game this week."

Not to be upstaged, JW jumped into the conversation. "Well, look at you, little darling. I'll be damned! I thought we were going to have to rent you some clubs, but I see you came prepared. I guess you know what you're doing after all."

Elizabeth smiled. She loved being underestimated.

Wickham glanced around. "Who else is coming?" he asked. His accent making the most ordinary words sound elegant and musical. Elizabeth decided she could listen to him talk all day.

JW replied, "First Thorpe bailed on us, and then Frank took off for a haircut." He glanced at Elizabeth. "I think our buddy Frank has an eye on your sister. Anyway, when he left, I had to grab one of the other guys who could play." And he looked around as he said, "Great, that's our boy now, coming down from the resort." Both Elizabeth and Wickham looked up to see Darcy Fitzwilliam heading their way. Elizabeth was still processing this fact when she heard Wickham groan.

She looked at him quizzically, but he quickly regained his composure and grinned at her. "Sorry, but that guy thinks too highly of himself." Wickham then leaned over and whispered in Elizabeth's ear, "He's kind of an arsehole."

Elizabeth giggled, partly because of the pronunciation of "arse" and partly because she didn't disagree.

Darcy approached, and Elizabeth couldn't tell if he was more dismayed to see her or George Wickham. He didn't immediately say anything, as if wondering how it was he'd found himself in this situation.

JW jumped in immediately. "Hey man, thanks for coming down. I take it you and Wick are acquainted?" He nodded over to Wickham. Wickham and Darcy gave each other a nod, but neither said a word.

JW continued, "And this little lady here is Elizabeth Austen. She's going to be joining us today. Better man up, Darcy; she looks like she could kick your ass." He chuckled.

Darcy cleared his throat and told JW, "We've actually had the pleasure of meeting." He gave Elizabeth a little nod. She managed to smile back, secretly disputing the word "pleasure" and JW looked at both of them curiously.

Wickham jumped into the first golf cart and waved JW over. "C'mon, mate, let's get this party started." He cracked a beer, and Elizabeth glanced quickly at her watch. It was only 9:00 in the morning.

She was forced to get into the other cart next to Darcy.

"Are you stalking me?" she teased, grinning up at him.

Then he did something she had never seen him do— he actually smiled, a full smile. He replied, "I really am sorry for that. Seeing you here caught me off guard. I was surprised, that's all. In case you haven't noticed, I'm not great with social interactions."

She considered this for a minute and then said, "Well

then, let's hope you're better at golf," a grin spreading across her face. "So, you know these guys?" she asked, curious as to how they were all acquainted.

"Yeah, as I shared with you, I've known Edmund since childhood, and our families are close. So I've met his buddies over the years." He looked pensive, as if debating whether or not to say more. Finally, he said, "I don't know JW too well, but I don't care for Wickham. We have some history…he's kind of an arrogant asshole."

Elizabeth let out a laugh, and Darcy looked over. "What's so funny?" he asked, looking wounded.

She smiled. "It's just that he said the exact same thing about you." Instead of looking angry, he gave her a lopsided smile. She felt her heartbeat quicken. What was it about his smile that caught her so off guard?

They pulled up to the tee and watched as JW and Wickham played through. She could tell JW was more at home on the course than Wickham, who had hit the ball awkwardly and hooked it toward the stream. He let out a string of expletives, and Elizabeth stifled a laugh.

She reached into her bag to grab her driver at the same time Darcy reached for his. Her hand brushed against his, which sent a jolt of electricity through her. She looked up and saw his gaze lingering on her, as she met his eyes she felt her cheeks flush.

Darcy quickly averted his gaze and moved aside. "Ladies first," he said.

She approached the mound, took a deep breath, brought the club back in one smooth motion, and with a powerful swing struck the ball, sending it straight down the middle. Darcy couldn't hide his admiration, and she saw him trying to stifle a grin. She watched as he, too, confidently approached the tee. He looked back at her, his brow furrowed and serious. He surveyed the course, drew back his club, and sent the ball cleanly down the green and within a few feet of her own ball.

Well, this just might be fun after all, she thought.

***

Elizabeth was enjoying herself out on the golf course. JW and Wickham had fallen into a relaxed, jocular mood that kept her laughing. They teased and made fun of each other, and it was obvious they liked each other's company.

It was quickly apparent that Wickham had little interest in the game. He took every opportunity to flirt with her. She liked him. He was charismatic, witty, and quick to smile, a sharp contrast to Darcy's serious and quiet demeanor.

"So, how do you know these guys?" Elizabeth asked when they found themselves together, waiting for a turn. She already had Darcy's explanation, but she was curious to hear what Wickham would say.

He leaned on his club and smiled at her. "I've known these blokes since college. Edmund and I shared a flat during his year at Oxford. Then, when I came out here for my last two years of uni, JW, Edmund and I roomed together. Great bunch of mates."

"And Darcy? How do you know him?" She watched as Darcy concentrated intently on the game, seemingly ignoring them.

At the mention of Darcy, she saw Wickham look over and watch him take his swing. His disdain was obvious. "One of Edmund's old mates. More family connection than friend. The bloke really knows how to kill a party. Look at him." He pointed his club at Darcy, who now seemed aware they were watching him and gave a scowl. Elizabeth couldn't help but smile, which caused his scowl to turn into a full-fledged frown. "That guy is a full-on buzzkill."

"He doesn't seem to like you much either," laughed Elizabeth.

"Hey, Wick, that ball ain't gonna hit itself into the sand trap! You're up," JW teased from the tee.

He grinned. "Excuse me, love. I've got to go teach these blokes a lesson." And he gave her a wink.

She couldn't resist a jab either. "You wouldn't want to lose your standing in last place," she giggled.

He made a point of brushing against her as he leaned over into his golf bag. "Well, I have been highly distracted today." He smiled back at her, his eyes lingering a little too long.

Elizabeth looked away shyly and caught a look from Darcy. His frown deepened. What was that guy's problem? Why did he even come out here if he was going to be in such a bad mood? She gave him a small wave and a smile and watched him look away uncomfortably.

But as the game went on, it became clear that only Elizabeth and Darcy cared about the outcome of the game. The other two were too busy goofing off, and they weren't very good in the first place. She liked Darcy's competitiveness. Watching him was making her more aware of her own game, more determined to beat him.

They were tied going into the last hole. She couldn't be sure from his expression, but she felt that Darcy was enjoying the competition as well. She was standing next to his clubs, and when he leaned over to grab one, his eyes fastened onto hers. They were so close she could feel the warmth of his breath on her skin. For a minute, she had the wild thought that he might kiss her.

He leaned in, his gaze sharp and unwavering. "Don't be fooled by his charm," he warned, nodding toward Wickham. "He's not a good guy."

"What are you, jealous?" she teased, still thinking they

were simply exchanging lighthearted banter.

But something in Darcy's expression shifted and a flicker of frustration darkened his eyes. "I don't know why I bother," he muttered, his tone edged with disappointment. Without another word he turned and walked away.

What the hell is this guy's problem? she wondered.

She poured her frustration into her last shot and beat him with a birdie to his bogey.

CHAPTER 10

Anne

"When pain is over, the remembrance of it often becomes a pleasure."

- PERSUASION

After breakfast, with Elizabeth headed off to the golf course and Elinor back at the room, Anne, Catherine, and Emma made their way over to the spa. Secretly, Anne felt a little wave of relief that it was only going to be the three of them. There was just more pressure when Elinor and Elizabeth were around. Anne felt more herself in the company of her two younger sisters.

They entered the peaceful quiet of the spa, and the scent of lavender and the sound of light music relaxed Anne immediately.

They were welcomed in by a young woman with a soothing, mellow voice. "Welcome to the Roman Bath Spa, ladies. A day of pampering and luxury awaits you." Then she stopped suddenly and let out a squeal, which echoed across the lobby of the quiet spa. She was looking adoringly at Emma. "Oh my god, is it really you? I know you! I follow you on Instagram!" she said excitedly, the calm, soothing voice all but gone.

Anne thought it was ironic. In a place like Mansfield Park, this young woman probably greeted powerful women every day without any clue who they were, but she recognized Emma from Instagram? She glanced over at her sister. Emma's long golden hair hung over her shoulders. She was wearing a bikini top and a wrap around her waist. A straw hat perched on her head, and her eyes were covered by large sunglasses. Anne realized her sister could pass for a movie star, and it occurred to her that no one would think twice about her belonging here.

The woman continued to gush. "My name is Harriet, and I just love your feed. I knew you were coming here from your post this morning, and I was like, 'I wonder if I'll see her,' and now here you are! You are even prettier in person."

Anne watched with amusement as her sister basked in the attention.

"Can I take a selfie with you, please? My friends are going to be so jealous! So like, are we *friends* now? Because I feel like I already know you, you know? Like your basically part of my daily routine. I wake up, check your stories-Oh wow, this is just so surreal, I should be recording this. You don't even know! This is literally the best day of my life. Like, I might cry," Harriet exclaimed, pulling out her phone.

As Emma interacted and posed with the young fan, Anne shook her head in bewilderment. She had no idea her sister was gaining this level of popularity, and it surprised her.

They moved toward the lockers, leaving a very happy Harriet to no doubt post the pic to her own feed.

What absolute craziness, thought Anne. Sure, Emma was beautiful and talented at what she did, but at the end of the day, she was just...Emma. The same sister who used to borrow Anne's clothes and leave dirty dishes in the sink.

Emma glanced over to catch both Anne and Catherine staring at her incredulously.

"What?" she asked, as if being accosted like a celebrity was a common occurrence. "So what do you think, hit the spa first, before our massages?"

"Ooh, do you think they have cucumbers to put over your eyes like in the movies?" Catherine asked. "I've always wanted to do that!"

Anne couldn't help but smile, appreciating Catherine's ability to find joy in the simplest of things.

At the lockers, as Anne began to put on her swimsuit, she glanced over at Emma and noticed that she was slipping on the spa robe with nothing on underneath.

"EM! You can't go into the water like that!"

Emma shot her sister a look. "Really, Anne? Now you sound like Elinor. There are no men here, and even if there were, who cares? It's so much more comfortable to go in the nude."

Catherine let out a little giggle, but Anne saw that she, too, was putting on her bathing suit.

As they entered the spa area, Anne looked around in wonder. An expansive central pool glistened under soft, ambient lighting. The pool was fed by gentle, cascading waterfalls that emerged from elegantly designed stone features. Plants were carefully curated throughout, with lush greenery draping over sleek pillars, adding a touch of nature while maintaining an elegant atmosphere. Surrounding the pool were lounge areas with plush seating and small tables that held bottled waters and hot towels. It was a complete water oasis.

Catherine squealed when she spied the tiny bowls of cucumbers. She took a seat and carefully placed them over her eyes. "Ah, this is the life," she sighed happily.

But after only a few moments she carefully set them aside.

"You guys go in. I'm going to relax and read for a bit," she said, pulling *Twilight* out of her bag.

"You're not reading that one where her boyfriend is the bloodsucking vampire again, are you?" Emma asked, shaking her head in disapproval.

"Don't judge Em, have you even read it? It's literally the best book ever. It has romance, drama, and vampires, it's perfect." Catherine answered, full of passion.

"Edward is a 100 year old dead guy who watches Bella sleep. That's called stalking, not romance," Emma said, laughing. "But you enjoy your reading sis. I'm ready for the hot tub."

Anne settled into the pool, feeling the heat of the water relax her entire body. She watched as Emma disrobed and looked around, relieved to see they had this pool to themselves. Emma carried her phone with her into the spa.

"Don't you want to leave that behind? Honestly, Em, you need to unplug for a while," Anne scolded her sister.

Emma sank into the pool and immediately took a few photos, then went to work on her phone to post them. "And pass up the opportunity to share this experience with my followers? Anyway, I'm considering this a working vacation. Despite Elinor's insistence that I don't have a job, this actually takes a lot of work."

She gave Anne a knowing glance. "And speaking of Elinor, she told me you are planning to enroll in a graduate program this fall," she said, obviously attempting to shift the topic away from herself.

Despite the relaxing nature of the water, Anne immediately felt herself tense. Damn it! It was just like Elinor to tell her sisters that Anne had decided on graduate school. She had, in fact, not decided at all. She felt her irritation with Elinor rising. Ever since Anne graduated college, Elinor had been pushing her to pursue a postgraduate degree. She knew that Elinor expected her to follow in hers and Elizabeth's footsteps to get a college degree, go on to graduate school, and then pursue a high-profile career. Anne didn't really know what she wanted. But instead of standing firm with Elinor, she had left it open ended and, apparently Elinor thought the decision was made.

Anne confided in her younger sister. "I know that's what she would like to see me do," she said hesitantly, "but I haven't made any decisions yet. Honestly, Em, I don't know how you convinced Elinor that you didn't need to go to college." Anne envied Emma's easy confidence and assertiveness, especially when it came to standing up for what she wanted. As much as Anne wanted to tell her older sister how she felt, she always backed down. How could she push back against Elinor, who had made so many sacrifices on behalf of her sisters?

Emma glanced away from her phone to catch Anne's eye. "Listen, I know Elinor wants what's best for us, but that doesn't mean she's always right, Annie. You need to learn to stand up for yourself, or you're going to end up living the life Elinor wants for you, not the life you choose."

Anne considered her sister's words. They stung because they were true, and this was not the first time Elinor had interfered in Anne's life.

"It's just that I'm content with my job right now," Anne said. And she meant it. When their hometown librarian, Mrs. Russell, retired, Anne was promoted to her position. She had been the school librarian for several years now and was actively involved in a literacy program for kids. The pay wasn't great, but it was a job she loved. She found it both satisfying and comforting.

"I'm happy for Lizzy and Elli. And Em, I'm thrilled that you're doing what you love, but I think I'm different. I know it would kill Elli to hear me say it, but sometimes

I think I'd be content to just settle down, get married, and have kids."

At these words, Emma sat up and exclaimed, "Oh Anne, that reminds me! Guess whose name I saw on the invite list?" But she didn't wait for her sister's response, she blurted out, "Frederick Wentworth! Wasn't that the name of the boy you hung out with all through high school? Isn't it wild that he would be here, of all places?"

Anne felt the breath go out of her. She hadn't heard Freddy's name for over seven years, and hearing it now made her heart beat faster. She was surprised to hear her own voice tremble as she spoke. "Frederick is coming here for the wedding?"

Emma had laid her head back in the water and closed her eyes again, oblivious to the turmoil she had caused in Anne's head.

"Actually, it's *Captain* Frederick Wentworth, to be exact—I'm assuming that's him. Can you even imagine Freddy as a captain in the Navy? I mean, no offense, Anne. I know he was your best friend or whatever, but he was kind of dorky. And whatever happened with you two? You were practically inseparable. I thought for sure you would keep in touch after he enlisted," Emma said.

"Oh, that was so long ago, Em. I lost interest long before he left, probably a good thing he went. I…barely remember him," Anne lied. She was glad that the heat from the spa could be blamed for the flush she felt across her face. Just telling the lie filled her with guilt. Because the truth was, Anne *did* remember him. She could never forget him, and she knew exactly what had happened between the two of them. Seven years ago, Freddy Wentworth had broken her heart

***

Anne couldn't relax for the massage. Her whole body

felt electrified. Emma casually mentioning that Freddy was here at Mansfield had set off an avalanche of thoughts in her head.

She remembered the summer she first met Freddy. It was the summer she turned thirteen; it was also the summer the sisters had lost their mother. The death of their mom had been a devastating blow to all them, and each had dealt with it in different ways. At nineteen, Elinor had been on the verge of going off to college at a renowned art school out of state. Instead, she decided to go to a community college near home so she could help their father with the younger siblings. Most of her time went into looking after Emma and Catherine, who, at ages nine and eleven, had needed the extra care.

Elizabeth, who was in her last year of high school, threw herself into her studies in preparation for college. But Anne was entering high school, and she felt completely lost without her mother's loving presence.

Every day that summer, she escaped to the library and read books all afternoon. Books were her sanctuary, a way for her to to escape her crushing grief. She could follow Alice down the rabbit hole or discover the worlds of Narnia, be anywhere but in her lonely world where her mother was gone.

Her daily presence in the library came to the attention of Mrs. Russell, the town's librarian, who took Anne under her wing and let her help around the library. It had been Anne's salvation, a place where she felt at home, something that belonged only to her.

Anne remembered when she had first seen the shy, withdrawn boy who also spent his afternoons in the library. His clothes always looked too small and his glasses too large, and he often appeared unkempt. She had often noticed him from across the library, always buried in a book, his fingers nervously adjusting his large glasses every few minutes. She had wanted to say something, to ask what he was reading, but she could never quite gather the courage.

But it was Freddy who made the first move. One afternoon, as she picked up the books near where he had been sitting, she found a folded-up piece of paper. It read, "I'm sorry about your mom."

Anne had felt a rush of tears sting her eyes. She glanced around the library for anyone else. But she knew this note had been left for her, and she knew exactly who had written it. She felt like he could see right into her heart and feel her grief.

That little note was all it had taken for a friendship to form. The next time he was in the library, Anne found the courage to talk to him.

She discovered that he wasn't as shy as he appeared. He had an easy manner about him that Anne found comforting. They could talk about almost any subject. They knew the same books, shared many of the same interests, and for the first time in her life Anne felt like someone was genuinely interested in what she had to say. With him, she could talk about how much she missed her mom and how it was hard to keep up with her high-achieving older sisters. She learned that, like her, Freddy had lost one of his parents at a young age. His father had died a few years prior, and his mother's remarriage to an abusive drunk made his home life unbearable. For him, the library had been a place of refuge as well. He wanted nothing more than to escape their small town and make a future for himself and she admired his quiet strength and determination.

As the years passed, their friendship blossomed into love and as graduation neared, their conversations took on a new intensity. Freddy knew what he wanted; he had waited all these years to get away from his family, and now it was time. He was going to join the Navy. The night before he was to leave for training, he had proposed.

"Come with me," he whispered, his voice filled with emotion. "Marry me, Anne."

Anne couldn't imagine her life without him, but she wasn't sure she was ready for marriage or to leave behind her own family. So she had turned to the two people she trusted most: Elinor and Mrs. Russell. Their strong objections, however, had both surprised and frightened Anne. Elinor in particular had thrown out all kinds of concerns, things Anne didn't want to think about. What if she moved with him and he changed his mind? What if she was passing up the opportunity to get her college degree? Did she want to be so far away from her sisters? Was she still too young to know her own heart? Marrying Freddy meant giving up her own life's plans, all for him.

In the end, they talked Anne out of it.

When she had told Freddy she couldn't marry him, the devastation in his eyes shattered her, but he had only nodded, jaw tight with emotion. "I'm leaving Anne," he said, his voice raw. "But don't expect me to wait around forever."

And she let him go, believing she was doing the right thing.

Anne knew her sisters had no idea how hard her first year at college had been. Only Elinor knew how serious their relationship had been, though she did not know of Anne's true despair at the breakup. Her other sisters had always assumed they drifted apart when he joined the Navy.

She dated a few men in her college years, but they only reminded her of what she had and what she had lost. She often found herself wishing she had followed her heart rather than her sister's advice.

Now, hearing that Freddy was here, she felt all the past pain resurfacing. Her mind was swirling. Why was he here? Would they run into each other? Did he hate her, and how would she bear it if he did? And, worst of all, had he married someone else?

***

"What's next?" Catherine asked, as they came out of their massages.

"Let's hit the pool. I need to freshen up my tan!" Emma said.

Anne looked at her sister's perfectly tanned complexion in comparison to her own pale skin and rolled her eyes in exasperation. "Please tell me you will at least put on a swimsuit for the pool," Anne said. Emma laughed but, to Anne's relief, slipped into her bikini.

"I could get used to this life," Emma stated as she sank into a beach chair, pulled her straw hat down over face, and began typing furiously on her phone.

Catherine pulled her beach towel over her head to create a little shade and settled in to read her book.

Anne applied a coat of sunscreen and tried to relax. She needed to get out of her head and think about something other than Frederick. She looked around, wondering who these people were who found themselves lounging by the pool at Mansfield Park on a random Wednesday afternoon. Her eyes followed an elderly gentleman hurriedly crossing the pool area. His wide-brimmed hat and sunglasses covered most of his face, and Anne noticed that his nose was generously lathered with white sunscreen. Despite the morning heat, he was bundled up in long sleeves and layers, as if he was heading out on an artic expedition. As he passed by, he shot her a disapproving scowl and muttered to himself about UV rays and skin damage.

Just then a couple arrived with their three small children interrupting the previously tranquil scene. They grabbed open chairs near Anne, and she and her sisters immediately overheard the wife complaining to her husband. "Charles, I simply can't understand why you would give the nanny a few hours off today. I've had to cancel my plans at the spa, and it's much too hot to be sitting out here by the pool," she whined.

Anne tried not to look like she was eavesdropping as she watched the young couple with fascination.

"Mary, I've already told you, she had a small emergency to attend to. But she's willing to come back this evening so we can attend the cocktail party. I'm sure you can manage your own children for a few hours. I've got my tee time now, but I'll meet you back at the suite in a few hours." He leaned over and gave his wife a peck on the top of her head. "Bye, kids!" he said giving the three small boys a wave as he hurried off.

The boys had eagerly stepped into the water. Anne watched them with an amused smile as they splashed each other with floaties on. Their mother looked less amused and seated herself more comfortably into the pool chair. She quickly found a fellow guest with whom she could restart her lament, and they became engrossed in conversation, one Anne was glad she could no longer overhear.

But she found she couldn't relax. It was obvious the young boys were unable to swim, and their mother was distracted and inattentive. She felt herself watching them keenly.

The youngest one had grown tired of his floaties and was now trying to pull them off. She anxiously glanced over at his mother, waiting for her to react, but she was too involved in her complaints and wasn't watching. In the blink of an eye, the youngest boy had removed his floaties and wobbled off the step, immediately immersing himself into the water.

Anne jumped up and dashed into the pool, pulling the

young boy to the surface. To her relief, she saw that he was just startled and had swallowed some water, but he was fine. The shock of it brought him to tears and finally got the attention of his mother.

She rushed over, taking the boy from Anne's arms. As soon as she saw he was okay, her concern turned to scolding, and he cried even harder. Flustered and annoyed, the woman rounded up her boys and led them away from the water, leaving Anne standing knee-deep in the pool.

The commotion had roused both Catherine and Emma, and they looked over to Anne with concern. As Anne moved toward the steps, she was approached by an older woman whose regal stature radiated a sense of confidence and grace.

"I saw what you did, and that mother is very lucky you were watching. I'm sorry she was too rude to acknowledge your actions. You were quite wonderful."

Anne beamed. "Thank you for your kind words. I really appreciate it."

The woman held out her hand to help Anne out of the pool. "I'm Sophie Croft; very nice to meet you."

Anne gave her a huge smile. "I'm Anne Austen, and I'm very pleased to meet you, Mrs. Croft. I recognized you, and I'm familiar with your husband's campaign. I'm actually a very big fan of yours."

The Crofts were a well-known couple in Kentucky politics. Admiral Croft had been a senator for the past four years and was now looking to run as the first Black governor of the state. His wife was well known in her own right, both for her political activism and for campaigning vigorously on behalf of her husband. One of her main projects was combating children's illiteracy, a cause near and dear to Anne's heart. Anne explained to her that, in her role as a school librarian, she had on many occasions promoted Mrs. Croft's programs.

"Well then, it sounds as if we have a mutual admiration

for each other," Mrs. Croft said graciously. "I hope we will meet again soon."

Anne felt pleased as she walked back to her sisters. "Well, look at you, saving lives and hobnobbing with senator's wives," Emma teased her as she returned.

She smiled. For the first time in a long while, Anne felt seen.

CHAPTER II

Catherine

"There is nothing I would not do for those who are really my friends.

I have no notion of loving people by halves, it is not my nature."

- NORTHANGER ABBEY

The afternoon humidity had made it too hot for her to read, and Catherine left her sisters out by the pool. She decided to head back toward the air-conditioned lobby. What she secretly hoped was that Henry Tilney might be working and she might "accidentally" run into him if she hung out near the front desk. She had no luck finding Henry, but she ran into Isabella.

Bella gave Catherine a large, easy smile and approached her. "I see you've got your book. How's the reading going?"

Catherine smiled in return. "I was out by the pool, but it's much too hot. I thought maybe I would come sit in the AC and get something cold to drink."

"Ooh, how about we grab lunch together? We have a great brewery on the other side of the gardens called the Pump Room. I get off in fifteen minutes; can I meet you there?" Bella asked eagerly.

Catherine felt a wave of gratitude for her new friend. She had enjoyed hanging out with her sisters this morning, but they weren't interested in the music or books that she loved. Having a friend her own age who was interested in similar things was an unexpected pleasure.

Plus, she still held out hope that hanging around Bella might lead to the opportunity of running into Henry.

"That sounds great. Let me change and I'll meet you there," Catherine answered happily.

Fifteen minutes later, she walked into the restaurant. She had been expecting a small bar, but the Pump Room was a large brewery with an outdoor pavilion and a view of the lake. It was a gorgeous location. She spotted Bella already sitting at a table, a pitcher of beer and two frosted mugs on top.

"I figured I would get us started," Bella said cheerfully and started to pour a glass for her.

Catherine thanked her and grabbed the mug. She didn't really like beer, but since Bella had taken the trouble to order it, she accepted it happily. She took in Bella's appearance and realized she was sporting a piercing in her nose, and her arms, now visible outside of her uniform, were covered in tattoos.

When Bella caught Catherine's glance, she smiled and said, "Yeah, this is the real me. The resort has a policy that we can't wear any face jewelry or have visible tattoos. It's so lame. Like half the people staying here have tattoos, so what's the big deal?" She took a large drink from her mug and rolled her eyes in exasperation.

"That is lame," said Catherine, eager to agree with her

new friend. She picked up her mug of beer and took a sip. She winced at the bitter taste.

The two of them fell into easy conversation. They discovered they both loved Taylor Swift's music and Timothée Chalamet's movies, and they could have talked for days on everything *Twilight.*

She loved being around her sisters, but she was envious of their ability to adapt to any social situation. Elizabeth was so passionate and opinionated, and Anne could talk on any subject with ease. Emma could fit in anywhere, and Elinor could listen to anyone. But Catherine struggled to keep up with conversations that bored her. It felt good to have a friend of her own, and she passed the afternoon chatting pleasantly with Bella.

As they finished up lunch and their third pitcher of beer, Catherine finally mustered up the courage to ask about Henry Tilney.

"So, what can you tell me about Henry?" she asked, hoping she sounded casual and only mildly interested.

"Henry?" Bella asked, puzzled. "Oh, you mean my boss?" She let out an exasperated sigh. "Oh, Catherine, you're not interested in him, are you? He's so...I don't know, he's just so goofy. Don't tell me you've come to Mansfield and set your sights on someone like Henry?" She shot Catherine a disappointed look. "The whole point of coming to a place like this is to find a rich guy, someone who can take you out on the town, spend money on you. You know, buy you things, take you places like this. I mean, that's why I'm working here. Everyone knows a wealthy man is just waiting for a woman to spend his money." She giggled, but Catherine knew she meant it.

It bothered her to hear Bella be so dismissive of Henry.

"I liked Henry, though. He seems more real than any of these men we see around the hotel. And besides, he's nice," Catherine said, not wanting to turn the subject away from him so soon.

Bella waved a hand dismissively "Nice is overrated, Cat. I want someone who can drop sixty dollars for a hamburger at lunch. By the way, thanks so much for picking up the tab. I've wanted to try this place ever since I started working here," she said, pouring the last few drops from the pitcher into her own glass.

Catherine felt flustered. She hadn't offered to pay, so why did Bella assume she would? The only thing she could think to say was, "You mean you've never been here before?"

Bella let out a dramatic sigh. "Of course not. I can't afford a place like this, just look at the check!"

The bill sat on the table and Catherine picked it up.

"Two hundred and forty-six dollars!" she gasped and looked at Bella in horror. "But we only had hamburgers and beer; how can this be right?! I can't afford this either. What are we going to do?" Catherine suddenly felt sick to her stomach.

Bella let out a laugh. "Of course you don't have to pay for it! You're on the Bertrams' tab this week. Just charge it to your room." Then she looked down at her watch. "Crap, I've got to get going, but this was fun! We'll have to do it again before you leave." She leaned down and gave Catherine a hug, and then she was gone.

All the good feelings from the afternoon evaporated, and Catherine felt like she might cry. This was exactly why her sisters always babied her; she was incapable of making good decisions. They would never have allowed themselves to get into this type of situation. How had she been such an idiot? Why couldn't she see Bella was taking advantage of her?

She felt angry with herself for being so naive. It had never even occurred to her how expensive the restaurant would be, and, even worse, she hadn't been assertive enough to ask for what she wanted. She didn't even like beer! She knew she didn't have to worry about the bill. Bella was right; she could charge it to the room and the Bertrams wouldn't even notice. But that just made her feel even worse.

Her spirits were low as she headed back to the suite, and on top of everything, she hadn't learned a thing about Henry.

CHAPTER 12

Anne

"Now they were as strangers; worse than strangers, for they could never become acquainted."

\- PERSUASION

"Really, Anne, that's what you're going to wear?" Emma said, appraising her sister through the mirror's reflection as she applied false lashes to her eyelid. "We are going to a cocktail party with distinguished guests, not a picnic." Now she was squinting with one eye and batting the lashes into place. "I mean, seriously, what were you thinking not bringing something more formal? Even Cat came more prepared than you," Emma scolded as she nodded over to Catherine.

Anne glanced at her youngest sister, wearing a stunning purple slip dress and hot-rolling her long hair into soft curls. She gave Anne a warm smile in the mirror, taking Emma's comment as a compliment rather than a slight.

Anne surveyed herself critically in the bathroom mirror. She glanced down at the piles of makeup and hair accessories her sisters had laid out across the bathroom's countertop. It was true; she hadn't given much thought about her appearance tonight. She'd slipped on a simple floral sundress, swept her hair into a messy bun on top of her head, and applied a quick coat of mascara. She grabbed one of Emma's red lipsticks, applied it liberally, and then, appalled at how garish it looked, quickly wiped it all away. She pushed her glasses up her nose and let out a loud sigh.

Elizabeth and Elinor's entrance into the room didn't make her feel any better. She had often heard her eldest sister complain about feeling frumpy, but Anne couldn't imagine why. Elinor carried herself with such poise and grace that she looked elegant no matter what she wore. Even Elizabeth, who rarely dressed up for any occasion, was rocking a pair of black dress pants with a yellow silk blouse and a single strand of pearls. How was it that around her sisters she always felt like the wallflower?

***

The sisters entered the veranda, which was already filling up with guests. The sun was low in the sky, casting a beautiful pink glow over the scene. Lights were just starting to come on, and the view of the grounds was stunning.

Anne took in the scene and immediately felt more relaxed. She took the opportunity to look around to see if Fanny and Edmund had made an entrance yet.

She heard him before she saw him. She would know Frederick's deep, gravelly voice anywhere, even after all these years. His voice had always attracted her to him. It lured you in. He had a way of making every conversation intimate, even when he was talking to a group of people.

Looking over to a small gathering of guests, she caught sight of him, and her heart beat wildly in her chest. She barely recognized him; he was so changed. His hair was now much shorter, cut in a military buzz. The silly little fuzz on his lip that he could barely grow at eighteen had turned into a full-scruff outline of a beard and mustache. His athletic build was in sharp contrast to the skinny boy she had once known and he had the healthy, tanned complexion of one who spent his time outdoors in the sun.

She couldn't take her eyes off him. Frederick Wentworth—*Captain* Frederick Wentworth, she had to remind herself, had aged remarkably well.

Her mind wandered back to the last time she had seen him- seven years ago. The memory was still so vivid. She could still see the hurt in his eyes when she told him she couldn't marry him, couldn't go with him, couldn't leave behind her sisters. She had believed, so naively, that their friendship would hold them together. She had pictured a future where, after she finished college, and he gained experience in the Navy, they would be ready for marriage.

At first his letters had come often, but they had soon stopped. She had wanted to reach out, but doubts filled her head and she was sure he had moved on and so her own letters went unsent. She became convinced that Elinor had been right, they had been too young and now out in the world, he had discovered a life that didn't include her.

She watched now as Frederick effortlessly entertained a group of guests. One of the young women laughed brightly, her eyes fixed on him with unwavering admiration. He seemed to be enjoying himself, telling his story with animation and expressive gestures. As he finished and chuckled, he looked around, took a sip of his drink, and his eyes caught Anne's. She saw the startled, confused look in his eyes. He stared for a moment, and she offered a smile and a casual wave. Anne held her breath, waiting for his own smile or wave or, better yet, for him to walk over and give her a friendly hug. But he just gave her a slight nod of acknowledgment and then returned his attention to his group.

There he was, standing just a few feet away, so close, yet unbearably distant. Once, he had been the person she knew better than anyone else, now he was a stranger, the years had erased everything they had been.

All the air left Anne's body; she felt faint. It took all her self-control not to burst into tears right there in the middle of the room. She turned away from him and locked eyes with Elizabeth.

"Anne, are you okay?" Elizabeth asked, leaning in to touch Anne's shoulder. Anne couldn't even manage the word "no," for she knew the tears were coming, so she walked unsteadily toward the exit.

Elizabeth followed Anne out of the room and into the large lounge inside the restroom.

"Anne, what is going on, hon? You have to tell me," Elizabeth asked, the concern clear in her voice. She leaned over and placed Anne's head onto her shoulder.

The tears finally came. They streamed down her face, and her whole body shook with grief. Elizabeth waited as she rubbed Anne's back and let the tears fall. Anne finally gained her composure and looked sadly up at her sister, her eyes red, her nose swollen.

"He's here, Lizzy, and he hates me." She could barely get the words out above a whisper.

"Who? Who is here?" Elizabeth asked, clearly baffled by her sister's distress.

"Freddy," she sobbed.

"Freddy? Wait, the boy you dated in high school? But you guys broke up so long ago; I don't understand," Elizabeth said, trying hard to grasp why she was so upset.

Then Elinor and Catherine entered the restroom lounge.

"Hey, Fanny will be here any minute! What are you girls doing in here? Come out, and let's go see her!" Elinor said, leaning over into the mirror to reapply her lipstick. It took her a minute to realize that something was wrong. "What's going on, you two? What happened?" she asked with concern as she turned away from the mirror.

Elizabeth responded for Anne. "I'm not sure I understand the situation," she said carefully, "but Frederick Wentworth is here, and it seems to have upset her."

All the commotion over the entrance of her sisters had given Anne a minute to compose herself. She did not have the energy or the inclination to share her feelings with them—and particularly not with Elinor.

She smiled weakly. "I'm okay," she said. "I was just caught off guard seeing an old friend. Lots of memories flooding back." She hoped this would satisfy her sisters, but she saw the look on Elinor's face and knew the questions would come later.

CHAPTER 13

Emma

"One half of the world cannot understand the pleasures of the other."

- EMMA

Emma was taking full advantage of the party, using it as an opportunity to network. So far she had chatted up an heiress, the granddaughter of a former president, and a luxury line entrepreneur. She was working the crowd, always on the lookout for potential sponsors or partnerships. And Elinor thought she didn't have a job!

She scanned the room and spotted Sophie Croft, the wife of Senator Croft, who had shown such kindness to Anne earlier in the day. Brimming with confidence and more than a few martinis, Emma introduced herself. A few minutes into their conversation, they were approached by a gentleman, and Mrs. Croft eagerly introduced them.

"Frederick!" She exclaimed and leaned over to give him a hug. "I'd like to introduce you to Emma Austen." Emma thought by Mrs. Croft's mischievous smile that she might be trying to play matchmaker. She turned to

Emma. "Emma, this is Captain Frederick Wentworth. He's going to be working on my husband's campaign."

Emma gasped. "Freddy!?" She would never in a million years have guessed this was her sister's nerdy crush from high school. He was nothing like the boy she had known, and she wondered what Anne would think when she saw him now.

Mrs. Croft replied with surprise. "Oh, you two know each other already?"

Emma replied enthusiastically, "Yes, Freddy and my sister dated in high school."

He smiled warmly at Emma. "It's great to see you, Emma. You've grown up a lot since the last time I saw you. How is your sister doing?"

Mrs. Croft sensing the conversation was best left between them, offered a polite excuse and walked away.

Emma recalled her earlier conversation with Anne at the pool and how disinterested she had sounded when she heard that Frederick was at the resort. Anne had not shared her thoughts with Emma, but Emma knew his being here bothered her, and she felt a protective surge for her sister.

"Anne is doing great!" she said with a bright smile. "She absolutely loves her job, stays busy with charity work, and she just started dated someone. Honestly, I don't think I've ever seen her this happy."

The part about dating someone had just popped out, but she felt good about it. That would send the signal that Anne was definitely not interested in rekindling anything.

"I'm glad to hear she is doing so well," he replied, and Emma thought she detected a hint of disappointment.

He looked as if he were about to say something else, but then they were interrupted by the arrival of Julia and Mariah Bertram.

"Emma, darling," Julia said, "we've been looking for

you all evening."

Frederick turned to Emma. "It was great to see you. Please tell Anne and your sisters hello for me." He gave a curt nod to Julia and Mariah, and then he, too, walked off.

"Who was that hunk?" Mariah asked, watching Frederick head back across the room.

Julia glanced down at her sister's ring finger, as if to remind her that she was no longer available. Mariah caught the look and gave her sister a big grin. "I was asking for you, of course." she said with a wink.

Judging by the expression on Julia's face, Emma suspected she wasn't buying it.

Julia turned to Emma, "Fanny and Edmund will be here any minute. We were hoping you and your sisters would head up with us to greet them as they arrive."

Emma had been so preoccupied that she had quite forgotten about her sisters.

"Of course," she said. "Only I don't know where my sisters have wandered off to. Let me-"

Before Emma could finish her sentence, Mariah called out across the room, "George! George, over here!" She was waving frantically at a very distinguished-looking gentleman, early thirties, with just a hint of silver starting to show at his temples. He appeared to be in conversation with some of the groomsmen.

He glanced over and gave Mariah a nod but didn't seem to be in any rush to respond to her frantic wave. When he caught sight of Emma though, he paused mid-sentence. He appeared to excuse himself from the group and walk over.

Mariah immediately looped her arm through his. "George, Julia and I need to head up to the entrance. Join us. We are expecting Edmund and Fanny any minute." She nodded towards Emma. "I'm sure you remember Fanny's cousin, Emma. She practically pestered you to death when we were kids."

He looked over at Emma and gave her an engaging smile, perhaps the one he had withheld from Mariah. "Emma Austen. The last time I saw you, you were stealing my horse!"

Recognition dawned on her then. "George Knightley, wow!" She smiled up at him. "I almost didn't recognize you; you weren't scowling and scolding me for something," she teased.

He let out a genuine laugh. "Like stealing my horse? You were always up to no good, Emma, and you were a terrible influence on my poor neighbors here," he said, waving toward Julia and Mariah.

"I didn't *steal* your horse; I just took him for a ride," she countered with a hearty laugh, remembering how mad he had been that summer when she talked Edmund into helping her saddle up George's beloved mare. "Don't tell me you still hold a grudge after all these years."

"Oh, I wasn't mad you took my horse, just that you went riding with Edmund instead of me," he said, teasing her back with a wink.

She felt a blush come to her cheeks.

Seeing him again took her immediately back to those summers spent at Fanny's home, and back to her childhood. She would never have admitted it to her sisters, but they had been right when they accused her of having a crush on him when they were younger.

"So tell me, Emma, what are you up to these days?" he asked, his eyes full of keen interest.

"I'm working for myself, creating social media content," she said proudly, but she immediately read the disapproval on George's face.

Mariah laughed. "Oh, you'll never catch George on social media. I doubt he even knows about Instagram or TikTok."

George shrugged his shoulders, "I've just never

seen the appeal of living out loud, I'd rather live in the moment. You miss out on too much when you're always on a phone. Just a personal choice."

Emma felt the wind leave her sails. Very few people could knock down her confidence, and she wondered why George Knightley was one of them. She wanted to tell him that she had over a million followers, that she had a lucrative contract with a major brand retailer, and that she had recently started her own online dating app, but she didn't think any of that was going to change his mind.

Mariah cut off any further conversation when she tugged at his arm. "Come along, George; we really must go find Fanny and Edmund." She turned to Emma. "Find your sisters and meet us up front."

George flashed his brilliant smile at Emma but put up his hand, as if to indicate there was no use arguing with her, and they walked off.

"You are a hard woman to catch alone," she heard a pleasant baritone say from behind her. Emma turned to see one of Edmund's groomsmen, the one who had approached their table at breakfast.

"I could say the same thing about you. Where is the rest of your posse?" she said, looking around for any other groomsmen.

"I told them I was coming over to talk to the prettiest woman in the room. But you've been very popular. I was hoping I could get you a drink?" He held up his glass, as if indicating she needed one.

"I'm sorry, but I don't think we've been formally introduced," Emma said smoothly.

He gave her a wounded look. "What! You've already forgotten this handsome face? We met this morning," he said, extending his hand. "Frank Churchill...again."

Emma laughed. "Well, Frank, I'm going to disappoint you for the second time. I need a rain check on that drink.

I've got to find my sisters and meet up with the bride and groom right now."

"A man can only take so much rejection. So I'm going to hold you to that drink, Emma." He gave her a wink and walked away. Emma thought she might just take him up on the offer, and soon.

She scanned the room and finally caught sight of her sisters, waving them over. "Where have you all been? You won't believe who I just saw—George Knightley! Can you believe it, after all these years? He's heading up front with Edmund's sisters. Come on, they're waiting on us. Fanny is here!"

CHAPTER 14

Elinor

"I will be calm. I will be mistress of myself."

- SENSE AND SENSIBILITY

Elinor was worried about Anne. She wasn't sure what had transpired before she entered the restroom, but she knew it was very unlike her sister to be so upset. The fact that Elizabeth mentioned it had something to do with Frederick Wentworth troubled Elinor even more.

It had been a long time since she'd thought about Anne's first boyfriend. Freddy was a common visitor to the Austen home during Anne's high school years. Elinor remembered the boy as being quiet and excessively polite. And always a little disheveled, as if no one at home took the time to remind him of his appearance or cared how he looked.

Elinor had never really given him much thought, other than feeling relieved that Anne seemed happy to have a friend to hang out with. So she was completely unprepared when, the summer Anne graduated, she came to Elinor stating Freddy wanted to marry her.

Elinor's initial reaction had been one of total dismay. Anne had been so studious in school; she had a scholarship to help cover college expenses and a job she enjoyed at the library. If she followed this boy, she would be giving all that up. Elinor knew Freddy did not have the means to support her sister. And what would happen if things didn't work out between the two of them? Where would that leave Anne?

In the end, Elinor had persuaded Anne to wait. If they were really in love, he could wait a few years, and in the meantime Anne could advance in her studies. The fact that Freddy had never returned only confirmed what Elinor had suspected all along—that they had been too young, and their feelings would change over time.

In all these years, she had never heard Anne speak of him again. So what could possibly have happened now to provoke such an outpouring of grief? The fact that Elinor didn't know what was going on with her sister bothered her deeply.

She was roused out of her thoughts by the arrival of Fanny and Edmund, whose entrance had drawn a crowd. Glancing over she saw Anne smiling and hugging Fanny. She seemed to be back to her normal self, and Elinor felt a sense of relief.

She watched as Fanny hugged and chatted with her sisters, surrounded by Edmund and all his family. It occurred to her that all of the guests here were Edmund's family, friends, or business associates of his father. She and her sisters were the only ones here for Fanny.

Elinor leaned over to give her cousin a big hug. Even with heels on, Fanny was still so tiny, and Elinor felt that pang again at how young she looked.

"You are positively glowing with happiness, and we could not be happier for you both," she said, leaning over to hug Edmund as well.

"We would have been happy with a small affair, but Father would not hear of it. So, here we are," said Edmund, sounding a bit overwhelmed by all the attention.

Fanny gave his hand a quick squeeze and a knowing smile. "We will just have to make the best of it," she teased. His loving smile in return removed any doubt Elinor might have had about their love.

She turned her attention to Edmund's family and took the opportunity to thank Mrs. Bertram for her kindness, sharing how grateful she and her sisters were for the accommodations for the week. Mrs. Bertram gave her an absent-minded nod and struggled to keep the wiggling pug in her arms still.

The sisters were also delighted to be reacquainted with George Knightley, who, they were informed, was to be Edmund's best man.

After an hour of pleasantries and casual conversation, Elinor felt herself grow weary. Anne and Elizabeth had disappeared again, and she watched as Emma and Catherine enjoyed themselves as they talked with some of the groomsmen. She wished she could feel lighthearted and fun like her younger sisters, but she never allowed herself to loosen up around strangers. She came across as too reserved, and it made her feel frumpy and old to hang out with the younger crowd.

The room had started to feel crowded and hot, and she slipped out onto the veranda to enjoy the cool summer evening and get away from the guests for a little bit. She loved the glow of the twinkling lights around the gardens, and she could hear the relaxing hum of cicadas.

She opened her phone, hoping to see a message from Eddie. Maybe he would use the pretense of having a work question, or maybe he would be bold enough to just ask how her evening was going. But there were no messages.

She sighed.

There were several tags from Emma's account, and she opened up Instagram to see what her sister had posted. As expected, Emma had posted *a lot* since they arrived.

Elinor watched one of her videos, which featured gorgeous pics from the resort's grounds. She had to admit, Emma really was good at this. She hearted a picture of the five sisters and felt a little guilty at how she was always scolding Emma for taking group selfies. The truth was, she was happy to have such great pictures of all of them together.

Unable to help herself she checked again for any messages from Eddie. Nothing. Without knowing what impulse had taken hold of her, she found herself pulling up Lucy's page on Instagram.

It technically wasn't stalking if her profile was open to the public, right?

The first post showed Lucy's beaming face holding one hand up to the camera with a huge diamond ring on her finger. Elinor froze. She forced herself to look down at the caption.

He finally popped the question, and I said yes, yes, YES!

Lucy was engaged? Elinor's heart pounded as she tried to process the news. If Lucy was engaged, it meant Eddie had formally proposed.

Her mind raced with all kinds of thoughts. She had been such a fool. Here she had been thinking they were starting to fall for each other. She had actually thought when he said he had "something to tell her" that he was going to confess his feelings. But she had misread the situation entirely. He had simply been planning to tell her he was going to marry Lucy.

Elinor pushed down the tears as she refused to lose control. She would not make a scene and have her sisters dote on her as they had for Anne earlier in the night. But she struggled to get control over her emotions.

Easing herself up, she avoided reentering through the main doors. Slipping around to the side entrance, she made her way slowly up to her room, hoping her sisters would still be down at the party.

She needed time to be alone with her broken heart and make sense of the emotions that threatened to overwhelm her.

CHAPTER 15

Elizabeth

"And your defect is a propensity to hate everybody."

"And yours," he replied with a smile, "is willfully to misunderstand them."

- PRIDE AND PREJUDICE

Elizabeth watched Fanny and Edmund make their rounds. They seemed so happy and in love, and she felt a small stab of regret at never having experienced that herself.

What was wrong with her that she was feeling so sentimental tonight?

Seeing her cousin so blissfully happy made her wonder what it felt like to fall in love.

She let out a long sigh, took a sip from her cocktail, and glanced around to pay more attention to who was present. She noticed Wickham across the room, in conversation with a petite brunette who appeared to be fawning over him and who, Elizabeth suspected, had too much to drink. He was making her laugh, and Elizabeth cringed at her exaggerated and overzealous giggles. Still, she felt just a little bit of jealousy as she watched him shower the brunette with attention.

Seriously, what was wrong with her tonight? Why should she be jealous that Wickham was paying attention to another girl?

She had to admit, he had utterly charmed her out on the golf course. Witty, charismatic, good looking, and, good lord, don't forget the accent, but jealous? Over him?

C'mon snap out of it, she told herself.

From across the room, Wickham met her eyes, gave her a boyish grin, and waved. She felt her cheeks blush as she gave him a small wave back. He leaned over to tell his companion something, then started walking toward her. The young woman shot Elizabeth a hateful look and watched as he approached.

"I was hoping I would see you here," he said. He gave her an approving look and raised his glass to her.

Elizabeth blushed with pleasure. "What about your friend over there? She doesn't look too happy," she said, nodding toward the young girl he had left so abruptly.

"That's just Lydia; she's fine," he said dismissively.

Elizabeth curious about the tension between Wickham and Darcy earlier in the day found herself asking him. "Care to share what was going on between you and Darcy this morning?"

Wickham visibly tensed. "We have some bad blood that goes back a few years," he said carefully. "I dated his little sister for a while in college. She was a real sweetheart...could have been something serious." He had a sad, wistful look in his eyes. "But Darcy put an end to it. He fed her some lies about me, and she broke it off. I mean, Edmund is still one of my best friends, but this type of wealth, these people, they all think they're too good for the rest of us."

Elizabeth could feel his frustration and anger, and she

felt a wave of sympathy.

"Do you know when Edmund asked me to be in the wedding, I actually turned him down? I mean, look at this place." His arms swept out around the room. "I'm not strapped for cash, but even I couldn't afford to stay here for a week. But Edmund wouldn't hear of it. He generously offered to pay for my stay; that's what kind of bloke he is. Then I heard Darcy tried to talk him out of it." He shook his head. "That's why I try to keep my distance from him."

Elizabeth immediately felt indignant on Wickham's behalf. Wasn't she in the same situation, after all? It was exactly what she and Emma were always arguing about—the superficialness of those who had money and their condescending attitude for those without. It just reinforced Elizabeth's feelings toward Darcy after their disastrous date. Now she finally understood what he meant by "not his type." It hadn't been a casual remark, it had been a declaration that he considered her beneath him.

His phone buzzed, and he looked down at it and glanced back up with a frown.

"Bloody hell," he muttered, giving Elizabeth a disappointed glance. "Sorry, love, but I've got to run. Save me a drink for next time?" His eyes lingered on hers for a long minute.

She felt her heartbeat quicken. "I'd like that," she said, trying to shake off her feelings of disappointment.

Once he'd gone, she sighed and turned toward the exit, only to catch sight of Darcy.

Speak of the devil! she thought. *But damn, this devil looked good.*

She had to admit, the man knew how to wear a suit.

She was still hot with indignation when he approached her.

But when he spoke, his voice was more tentative and

nervous than she had ever heard it before.

He cleared his throat. "Elizabeth, I was wondering if you would have dinner with me tomorrow after the races?"

The question took her aback. Was he really asking her out right now? The conversation with Wickham was still fresh in her mind.

Oh, so now that she was staying at Mansfield he'd deemed her "worthy" of a date?

She scoffed. "Let me get this straight, Darcy. You dumped me on our first date, accused me of stalking you, and spent an entire day ignoring us. And now you want to take me to dinner?" Her indignation made her feel bolder.

He stiffened and stood straighter. "And who, exactly, are you referring to when you say 'us'? You and Wickham? I thought I already explained to you that he and I have some history," he said, his own anger and frustration now present. "He is not someone I choose to associate with. I thought you understood that."

"Exactly! Thank you for proving my point," she snapped and turned to walk out of the room. She felt a sense of satisfaction at the completely baffled expression on Darcy's face.

CHAPTER 16

Catherine

"And are you prepared to encounter all the horrors that a building such as "what one reads about" may produce? Have you a stout heart? Nerves fit for sliding panels and tapestry?"

- NORTHANGER ABBEY

Catherine was so bored. She looked around the crowded room that still bustled with guests caught up in conversations, drinks and hors d'oeuvres. She took in the hum of low voices. She knew many of the guests were people of importance who were using the gathering to network or advance their cause.

After Fanny's arrival, she lost track of each of her sisters. Elinor had long left the ballroom. Catherine had enjoyed hanging out with Emma for a while, but it was clear Emma wanted to do some networking of her own. Anne was much more skilled at keeping up with political conversation and had no trouble holding her own in polite company. She couldn't remember the last time she had seen Elizabeth.

She looked around and felt like she was probably the youngest in the room, with the exception of the bride. She sighed. Would anyone even notice if she left at this point? She made the decision to head back to the room and maybe sink into a hot bath with her book before her sisters came back to the suites. The thought of having a few minutes to herself immediately brightened her spirits. She snuck one last look around the room and, confident she would not be missed, slipped out into the hallway and headed back toward the lobby.

As she started to head up the grand staircase, she caught sight of Henry. He spied her as well, and a smile lit up his face.

"Catherine, right?" he asked.

"Yes, and it was Henry, wasn't it?" she replied, but she knew full well that was his name, as she had thought of little else over the past day.

"Party over already?" he inquired.

"No," she admitted, a little embarrassed. "I just...well, you know, I don't have much in common with anyone, and my sisters seem occupied, so I thought I'd head back to the suite."

"Ah, so you have a date with a pale, brooding, mysterious man?" he asked. His eyes had a mischievous glint to them.

Confused, Catherine stammered, "No, I-I don't have a date!" But then she realized he was teasing her, referring to Edward from her novel. She grinned. "Well, I guess I was hoping to spend the evening with a handsome vampire."

"So what else do you like to read besides vampire romances?" he asked.

"I love murder mysteries and true crime. Oh, but my favorite is gothic horror. Give me a decrepit castle or abandoned mansion on a stormy night, throw in the supernatural, dark family secrets and a grisly murder and I'll be happy for days."

She looked up and caught Henry watching her intently. "What?" she asked self-consciously, running a hand over her nose and mouth in case there was something on her face.

He immediately let out a long laugh. "I'm sorry, I was just enjoying watching you get so excited about horror. It was cute...scary, but cute." His grin grew wider.

Catherine blushed and smiled. "Yes, my sisters tend to worry about my obsession, especially when I share details on how to get away with the perfect murder."

Henry laughed again, and Catherine felt her heart beat faster. She had never felt so comfortable being herself around anyone. She never thought of herself as interesting or funny. She knew she tended to take people too literally, but Henry seemed to be genuinely enjoying her. She had even been able to make him laugh.

"How about you? What do you do when you're not working here?" she asked.

"Sorry to disappoint, but I have no secret life as a vampire. I'm afraid I mostly study. I'm in my third year at Kentucky University."

"So am I!" she exclaimed.

Henry looked surprised. "I guess I just assumed when you checked in that you were coming from out of state," he said.

She gave a little laugh. "And I assumed you were long out of school."

"Ouch, that hurt," he said, pretending to grab his heart and sway a little.

She giggled again; she really did find him irresistible. They were both quiet for a moment, and she suddenly realized he was still in his work uniform.

"Am I keeping you from work? I don't want you to get

in trouble," she said, concerned.

"No. As a matter of fact, I just got off," he replied.

All of a sudden, the thought of going back to the suite was a little less appealing.

Henry got a twinkle in his eye. "I think I have an idea. I'll tell you what: give me a few minutes to change out of my work clothes and, if you want to put on something more comfortable, I'll meet you back here in ten minutes. Deal?" he asked, extending his hand out to Catherine to shake.

When she clasped it, she felt her pulse quicken.

"Deal!" she said, rather breathlessly. "I'll meet you back here in ten minutes."

She wasn't sure what he could possibly have in mind, but she didn't care. She raced back to her suite, threw on a pair of jeans and a sweatshirt, and raced right back down.

***

When she reentered the lobby a few minutes later, Henry was there waiting for her. It was the first time she had seen him out of his hotel uniform. He was leaning up against the wall, looking casual and relaxed in jeans and a black tee. He gave Catherine a wide grin and held up his hand. Something was dangling from his fingers. She realized it was a hotel room key, and disappointment immediately washed over her. She blushed.

"I-I'm sorry, Henry, if I gave you the wrong idea," she started to stammer. "I didn't mean to lead you on. I really can't—"

Henry let out his boisterous laugh and beamed down at her. "No, I'm the one who's sorry. I should have explained. This key opens Room 813. Surely you've heard of Room 813 at Mansfield Park?!"

Catherine shook her head, confused. "No, what is so special about Room 813?"

Henry leaned over and whispered into Catherine's ear, "It's haunted."

Catherine felt a shiver, she wasn't sure if it was from his words or the closeness of his presence.

"Go ahead; Google it!" he told her.

She looked him square in the eye, trying to find any clue about whether he was just trying to tease her, or if he was serious.

His look was intense, and he nodded at her phone. "Go on," he said.

She pulled out her phone and typed in "Room 813," and immediately she saw the browser complete the search with "Mansfield Park." She hit the search, and the headline read, "*Lady in Blue Haunts Popular Resort.*"

The article told the story of a young woman in the 1920s who was said to have been meeting a lover at the hotel but was stabbed to death by her jealous husband in Room 813. Guests who have stayed in the room over the years have reported eerie encounters. Stories of soft whispers in the night, flickering lights, and a feeling of coldness to the room, kept Catherine reading with rapt attention. When she finished, she glanced up to find Henry smiling at her and dangling the key again.

"So, shall we go check out Room 813?"

She felt a thrill of excitement. "Oh yes, let's go!"

As she started to follow Henry, she realized that she hadn't told her sisters where she was or what she was doing. She thought of all the young women from her true crime novels. What was she doing going anywhere with a complete stranger? She suddenly felt very foolish and stopped abruptly. Henry turned and caught her worried expression.

"Is there something wrong?" he asked. He looked so

concerned that Catherine wondered how she could even suspect him of anything untoward. Then her mind flashed again to stories like those of Ted Bundy. Henry seemed to read her mind.

"Do you want to let someone know where you are going?" he asked.

Catherine relaxed. "Yes, I think I ought to let my sisters know who I'm with."

She typed a quick text to Anne. *Left party, hanging out with Henry.*

Anne's reply came immediately. *Who is Henry????*

Catherine looked at him. "Do you mind if I send her a pic?" she asked shyly as she held up her phone.

Before he could respond, she snapped a quick picture. He peered over to look at the out-of-focus snapshot.

"I don't mind at all, but please make me look more handsome than that!" he laughed. With that, he leaned his elbow on the stair railing and rested his fist under his chin. "How's this pose?"

Catherine giggled, then snapped the picture and glanced down at the image. It made her smile, and she was secretly happy to have a picture of him to look at later. She sent it off to Anne with a quick text. *This is Henry. Pretty sure he's not a killer but sending this pic just in case.*

As she put the phone back in her pocket, Henry said, "All set?" and gave her a big smile. Then he reached over to hold her hand as he led her to the elevator.

The eighth floor looked similar to the second floor, where she and her sisters had their suites, but here the hallway seemed longer, quieter, and darker. She felt a shiver of anticipation.

"Is 813 still used for guests?" she asked Henry, feeling a need to break the silence.

"No. After several years of complaints, management took it out of commission. But it's available upon request, which we see from time to time. Ghost hunters, podcasters, they've all stayed here. It's popular around October, and it's always booked for Halloween. But most of the time, it's just a vacant room."

She watched him as he took the key out of his pocket and turned it in the lock. He turned toward her, his gaze intense, and raised one finger to his lips. They moved into the room slowly, Catherine squeezing his hand more tightly. She was certain that her heart was beating so loudly Henry could hear it. He switched on the light, and Catherine's eyes swept around the room.

It was a large suite, with a bed along the wall, a small sitting area, and a balcony that faced out onto the golf course. She both relaxed and felt a little wave of disappointment. There was nothing here that gave the appearance of anything sinister or scary. She glanced at Henry.

"What should we do now?" she asked.

He put a finger to his lips again and whispered, "Shhh, she doesn't like anyone talking in her room."

Catherine didn't know whether he was being serious or teasing her again, but she didn't ask another question.

Henry sat on the edge of the bed and patted it for her to join him. Then he began to recount the story in a low, hushed tone.

"Close your eyes. Imagine this place a hundred years ago. It's the 1920s. The era of Prohibition, speakeasies, and gangsters. And, much like today, Mansfield was full of people with money and secrets. It's rumored the hotel was used by bootleggers as a temporary holdover for cases of alcohol that would eventually be distributed throughout the state."

Catherine closed her eyes. She could easily conjure up the world Henry was painting.

"Now, picture our beautiful victim. A naive young woman who unwittingly found herself married to a notorious mobster. It wasn't long before he displayed his true character and cruelty, and she realized she had made a terrible mistake. When she met one of her husband's business associates, she fell madly in love. Desperate to flee her unhappy marriage, she made plans to run away with him. Dressed in a flowing blue dress, cheeks flushed with excitement, eager to meet her lover, she checked into this very room."

Catherine opened one eye and glanced around, whispering, "She probably sat on this very spot."

Henry continued, "Unfortunately for our poor young heroine, she had terrible taste in men, for her lover had duplicitous motives in setting up their rendezvous. Driven by his own greed, he informed her husband of the planned meeting in exchange for money. That fateful night, as she opened the door with breathless anticipation, her smile faded into a scream. Instead of her lover, her cruel husband stood before her, his jealousy and rage casting the final shadows on her young life."

Catherine gave an involuntary shudder.

"According to the police report, they found her disfigured body the next morning. She had been stabbed repeatedly and strangled. The scene was described as particularly gruesome, with bloodstains on the bed and carpet and spatters up the wall. Since that fateful night, she remains, a spectral silhouette in blue, forever re-living the horror of that endless night, waiting for a love that will never return."

Henry's voice dropped even lower, just above a whisper. "Some say, if the night is still, you can hear the rustle of her dress and her whispering sobs echoing through the halls, a chilling reminder of her tragic betrayal and eternal vigil."

As he finished his story, Catherine felt another shiver run up her back. Was it her imagination, or had the room just grown a little colder?

She glanced over at Henry. She thought he looked a little nervous too.

"I think we are safe from the Lady in Blue tonight," he whispered, but just as he said it, a loud thud came from the unlit bathroom. They both looked at each other, unsure of what they'd just heard.

"Let's get out of here," he said, and just as Catherine stood up to follow him, the overhead light flickered, and then darkness fell across the room.

She wasn't sure who ran faster, but they both made for the door and stumbled out into the dimly lit hallway, slamming the door behind them. They caught each other's eye and saw the mutual terror, and then they both burst out laughing.

"Well, that's enough of a scare for one evening," Henry said, his voice trembling just slightly, and for the second time that night he grabbed Catherine's hand. They walked a few paces past the door and then started running down the hallway, laughing the whole way.

"I need a drink after that, care to join me?" he said, glowing with the rush of adrenaline.

"As long as it's not beer," Catherine replied, remembering her distaste for it after her afternoon spent with Isabella.

"Hmmm…I think I know what will hit the spot. Trust me enough to follow me one more time?"

She managed a weak, "Yes." She knew she would follow him anywhere.

This time, they found themselves in one of the smaller kitchens. There was only a handful of hotel staff, and they all seemed to know Henry, giving him waves and smiles as he walked her through. He pulled out a huge tub of ice cream from the freezer and picked up a scooper. He dished up two big scoops into glasses and then opened the fridge to pullout two cans of root beer. He looked over at Catherine with a serious expression on his face. "Now the key to a great root beer float is getting the right ratio of ice cream to root beer."

She watched as he filled the glasses until they were full with foam covering the tops, and then handed one over to her.

"So, what did you think of your first ghost adventure?" he asked, his lip covered in ice cream and foam.

Catherine smiled radiantly. "Best night ever," she replied.

"Not quite…it's just missing one thing." He leaned over and whispered, "May I kiss you?"

She lowered her spoon and gave a small shy nod. He closed the space between them and lightly touched his lips to hers. Then he pulled her closer to him and kissed her longer, deepening the kiss and tasting deliciously of root beer and vanilla ice cream.

CHAPTER 17

Elinor

"Pray, pray be composed, and do not betray what you feel to everybody present."

- SENSE AND SENSIBILITY

E linor heard her sisters come in at all different hours after the party last night. When the evening started, she had hoped they would all have some time to catch up. But after seeing Lucy's post, she had no desire to be in anyone's company, worried that her feelings would betray her.

She had often spoken of Eddie to her sisters in passing. They knew him as one of her clients, one of the many authors she worked closely with. She had never hinted at her growing feelings for him. She wasn't even sure she had understood her own feelings until last night. She knew Eddie had a commitment, an obligation, but she had still allowed herself to hope. Now all that disappointment was crashing down on her. And yet she did not feel she could share her true feelings, not even with her sisters.

She braced herself for a long day ahead. They were to

spend the day at the racetrack. The Bertrams had reserved a large balcony and several boxes for the guests to mingle and watch the races. Elinor knew she had to put Eddie out of her thoughts for the day. This was Fanny's time, and she did not want her feelings to intrude on the happiness of the occasion.

Emma poked her head into Elinor and Elizabeth's suite, dressed in a red slip dress, made of thin material, and a large red derby hat. Elinor looked at her sister admiringly. She looked stunning.

"What! You're still in bed? You better get moving; we need to be downstairs in thirty minutes."

"You look amazing!" Elinor said with genuine feeling. "I didn't realize we were dressing up for the races. I didn't bring anything."

Emma smiled big. "I figured as much. That's why I brought a surprise for y'all. The pay might be crap, but as I said before, the perks of this job are great...free clothes. I brought an outfit and a hat for each of you, tailored just to your sizes. The Austen sisters are going to make a fashion statement today. Now, come on; everyone else is almost ready," she said, full of enthusiasm.

She brought forth a beautiful blue floral print dress on a hanger with a large dark blue hat. "I picked blue just for you, Elinor. To match your eyes."

Elinor started to protest, but she took in the dress and knew at once it was going to look amazing on her.

Elinor emerged twenty minutes later to find her sisters dressed for a day at the races in the outfits Emma had picked out especially for them. Catherine beamed in a pink gingham sundress and adjusted her small pink hat as she surveyed herself in the mirror

"I think I look like Reese Witherspoon in *Legally Blonde*," she said, giggling.

Elinor thought she looked beautiful. The gingham

made her look especially young, and her strawberry locks cascaded down from her small hat.

"You are totally pulling off the Elle Woods vibe," Elizabeth teased. "We just need to borrow Mrs. Bertram's pug to complete the look!"

Emma had picked out a lovely yellow, A-line sundress with a matching hat for Anne. It flattered her curves and accentuated her dark hair and eyes.

"Anne, that dress looks fantastic on you, and Lizzy, you look fabulous in that color," Elinor added, eyeing Elizabeth, who was in an emerald-green pantsuit with a beautiful green silk fascinator.

Elizabeth smiled. "I'm just so happy Emma knows me well enough to not get me a dress! It's bad enough I have to wear one for the wedding," she said, smiling approvingly at her reflection in the mirror.

Elinor marveled at how Emma had picked the colors and outfits that suited each sister perfectly. She felt a wave of appreciation for her sister.

"Selfie time!" said Emma, positioning her camera to catch the gardens in the background. "Crowd in, and Elli try to keep your eyes open this time." Elinor sighed, appreciation quickly fading to annoyance.

***

An hour later, they found themselves in a box suite with an expansive view of the racetrack below. The balcony was crowded with guests from the hotel, but Elinor felt as if she had walked into a fashion show. The women were dressed in bold style statements, wearing the biggest hats with everything from flowers to feathers attached. Elinor again felt grateful to Emma for thinking of them. For once, they fit right in.

Even the men were dressed for the occasion. Most

were in suits and ties, some even in tailcoats and top hats.

Elinor started to relax and enjoy the festive atmosphere. She glanced around for any familiar faces and was pleased to see George Knightley striding their way followed by two guests she didn't recognize.

"When did George turn into the sexy professor type?" Elizabeth said a devilish grin on her face.

"Lizzy!" Elinor exclaimed, appalled but unable to hold back a laugh.

"What?" Elizabeth feigned a look of innocence. "I'm just saying with that authoritative voice, those thoughtful eyes, the beard…he totally gives off 'hot teacher' vibes."

"Eww, isn't he old?" Catherine asked

Elinor looked at her youngest sister with exasperation. "Really Cat! He's my age."

"I know, like I said, old," Catherine grinned.

"What I want to know, is who is that couple he's talking to and what is that tacky woman wearing?" Emma said distractedly, posing herself for a selfie, the racetrack in the background.

"So, you have noticed something other than what's on your phone," Anne piped in.

"I always notice fashion and that woman's dress is a dupe and the purse a knock off," Emma said without even looking up from her phone.

All conversation between them ended abruptly with the arrival of George Knightley and the couple.

"Ladies," he said, giving them all a warm smile. "You all look very beautiful today, and festive. I'm glad I found you all together, as I would like to introduce you to the Reverend Elton and his wife, Augusta. Reverend Elton will be performing the ceremony for Fanny and Edmund on Saturday." To the Eltons, he introduced each of the sisters as Fanny's cousins and bridesmaids.

The reverend gave them all a gracious but uninterested smile. His wife appeared haughty and even more disinterested. As the waiter passed their group with a plate of hors d'oeuvres, she snapped her fingers at him.

"Yoo hoo! Yes, you, young man, please bring those over here. I'm simply starved. I have to say I've been rather disappointed in our stay at Mansfield. The food is simply atrocious. Don't you agree Georgie?" She looked up expectantly at Knightley.

"I've had no complaints Augusta," he said smoothly, and Elinor thought she detected a forced politeness.

Mrs. Elton continued undeterred. "Frankly, I expected more from Mansfield. Of course, we've just come back from our honeymoon, and I think we must have been spoiled by our stays in Paris and *Venezia*—that's how the Italians pronounce it," she said looking around with a self-satisfied air.

As Mrs. Elton rushed into sharing details of their trip, Elinor noticed Emma had begun taking selfies again and wandered away from the group.

Catherine had casually wandered off and Elizabeth and Anne managed to excuse themselves, but Elinor felt it was rude to leave the conversation. Damn it, how was she the one who always got stuck? She looked up, nodding graciously as Mrs. Elton continued to lament the difference between European and American hospitality.

"And our room at Mansfield. Well, I have to say, it's nothing to write home about. Wouldn't you agree, Ms. Austen?"

Elinor couldn't imagine anyone not being impressed with the grandeur of the resort, so she answered as diplomatically as she could. "Well, I have to say, we are quite happy with our suite, and the view of the gardens is delightful."

Mrs. Elton's face fell. Her mouth was full of a stuffed mushroom, and little pieces went flying out as she spoke. "A suite! You have a suite?" She turned to her husband, indignation raging in her eyes. "Philip! Philip, did you hear that? I just don't see why the bridesmaids get a suite but not the most important person in the wedding party!"

Elinor couldn't help but think that the bride and groom were the most important ones, but thought better of saying it out loud.

Mr. Elton now spoke up for the first time. "Outrageous! I agree, Augusta. I'll speak to Edmund and get this cleared up. An oversight on the part of some clerk, I'm sure."

This seemed to appease Mrs. Elton, and she glanced around for another waiter to flag down. Elinor took the opportunity to discreetly excuse herself.

Once again, she couldn't help but worry for Fanny and the world she was about to marry into.

CHAPTER 18

Emma

"It was badly done, indeed!"

- EMMA

Emma had found Mrs. Elton to be insufferably boring and felt no qualms at leaving Elinor to keep her occupied. Her elder sister was good at that. Elinor had a patience for tiresome people that Emma just didn't have.

She glanced up from her phone to find George Knightley smiling and studying her.

"Do you make it a habit to pick up your phone in the middle of conversations with people?" he asked and from his tone she wasn't sure if he was teasing or scolding her.

"Only when they are horribly uninteresting," she replied, making a point to slip her phone into her purse. "And did that tacky woman really call you Georgie?"

He gave a soft chuckle. "The Eltons definitely think highly of themselves. I'm afraid being asked to officiate such a high-profile wedding has only inflated that sense of importance. But I appreciate your indignation on my behalf."

She had felt indignation on his behalf. George Knightley was a man who carried himself with professionalism and confidence. He was obviously someone comfortable in a business meeting or board room. And she was pretty sure he was a man more accustomed to being addressed as Mr. Knightley rather than Georgie.

His blue eyes held hers for a moment but then his attention was diverted by the arrival of two lady guests. The younger of the two women was tall and beautiful, and Emma was immediately struck by her poise. Wearing a white pantsuit with a large black-and-white striped hat, she had an Audrey Hepburn quality about her, and Emma felt that familiar sting of jealousy. The older woman was more shabbily dressed, and Emma tried to suppress a giggle at her hat, which had what appeared to be fake fruit piled up high on the brim.

Knightley smiled big and greeted them both graciously. "Jane Fairfax, how lovely to see you."

She smiled brightly and replied somewhat timidly, "It's wonderful to see you too. George, let me introduce you to my aunt, Ms. Bates."

Jane's aunt immediately took this as her cue to start talking. "Oh, how fun is this! I'm just thrilled to be here. Jane is such a sweet girl. When she received an invitation to the Bertram wedding, you know, well, I just couldn't believe my luck that she would ask me to come along. Such a sweet girl. Of course, her mother's been dead for six years now, and I'm really the only living relative she has, but still, she could have brought anyone. However, she knew I'd never been anywhere like this, and I'm just so thrilled to be here. Jane really is such a sweetheart, and talented too. Did you know she occasionally plays piano for the philharmonic orchestra? I mean, they don't always have a piano, but when they do they call on my Jane. She plays quite beautifully. Like I said, such a talented girl."

Emma groaned inwardly. How had she ended up trapped in yet another boring conversation? She listened impatiently to Ms. Bates ramble on. Jane, for her part, looked mildly uncomfortable at her aunt's profusive praise.

Emma fought the urge to pull her phone out but was keenly aware of George's recent admonishment. Instead, she yawned rather loudly. She caught the look of disapproval flicker across George's face.

OMG, will this woman ever shut up? She chided herself for being unkind, but the woman was beyond annoying.

"We came straight from the resort this morning—no time to even grab a bite to eat. We are just famished!" Ms. Bates continued to beam.

Before she could think better of it, Emma blurted out, "Well, maybe you could just pluck a piece of fruit from your hat." She instantly regretted it when she saw the horrified expression cross Ms. Bates's face. The elderly woman flushed with embarrassment and immediately went quiet.

Jane, too, looked horrified and said gently to her aunt, "Perhaps it would be a good time to go find something to eat, Aunty." She glanced over at Emma. "Nice to meet you, Emma, and always a pleasure to see you again, George," she said, and before Emma could even acknowledge the goodbye, the women had walked away.

George Knightley immediately faced her, "Really, Emma? Just when I thought you've finally grown up, you go and do something like that." It wasn't anger she read on his face but disappointment.

Emma started to protest. "But I mean, really, she wouldn't stop talking about her niece and—"

He cut her off. "Emma, you embarrassed that poor woman. It was obvious she was uncomfortable and out of her normal element. Would it have hurt you to show a little patience and kindness?" He gave an exasperated sigh. "I hope you will find her and apologize, now if you will excuse me." With a curt nod he walked away.

Emma felt shame rush over her. Her mouth had moved faster than her brain. She'd intended for it to be funny, not hurtful. Worst of all, she felt she had disappointed George, and she didn't know why this bothered her so much. Why did he always have to make her feel like a little girl again?

She looked around the room, hoping to see her sisters and regain a bit of her composure. Instead, she spotted Mariah Bertram heading her way. Mariah moved with the effortless grace of someone who never doubted their own importance.

"Emma! Well, don't you just look adorable," she said, and Emma couldn't decide if it was sarcasm or a genuine compliment. She reached over and gave Emma a hug and an air kiss on the cheek. Mariah wasn't Emma's favorite person, but after the Eltons and Ms. Bates, she was actually relieved to see her.

"You look like the belle of the ball," Mariah said, appraising Emma's red dress and matching red rose hat with approval. Emma beamed at the compliment. It was rare for Mariah to admit that anyone met her standards.

"Em, doll, I need a favor," she said as she looked out over the balcony.

And that was the catch, thought Emma.

"Fanny's wedding planner is the most odious man." She drew out the word "odious," enunciating all three syllables. "And, unfortunately, he's trying to track me down today." She looked furtively around the crowd. "Mother gave us free rein over most of the wedding decisions. I mean, since Fanny clearly had no idea what to do. Except she positively insisted on using Mr. Collins as the wedding planner. Apparently, he came highly recommended by mother's good friend, Ms. de Bourgh, and he did do such a beautiful job with the Weston wedding last year. They rather forced our hand on this one. Anyway, I'm sure he will be worth the trouble, but he is so horrifyingly boring."

Emma looked at Mariah expectantly, wondering how she could possibly help.

"Well, I was hoping you could provide assistance with the seating arrangements for the rehearsal dinner. He is asking how we want to pair up the bridesmaids and groomsmen for the walk down the aisle and table seating. Anyway, I thought you could help him, and it would give me a chance to sneak away." She gave Emma her brightest smile.

As if on cue, Emma heard someone behind them clear their throat, and they both jumped. She whirled around to see a man she assumed to be Mr. Collins.

He was very well-dressed, short, and had a mustache that could rival Hercule Poirot—but all of that was overshadowed by what was possibly the worst toupee Emma had ever seen. Its black strands were a sharp contrast to the man's receding gray hair underneath, giving the whole thing an unnatural look. It sat atop his head like a misplaced rug. Emma resisted the urge to reach over and straighten it for him. As he spoke, it shifted awkwardly, revealing patches of bare scalp. Emma could barely peel her eyes from the top of his head.

He glanced up at Mariah and said, "Oh, thank heavens I've found you, Miss Bertram. I've left several messages for you and the other Miss Bertram. I can only assume that your many duties and obligations have not afforded you the opportunity to return my calls. I understand you wanted to make some minor changes to the seating and flower arrangements?" Here he took a moment to catch his breath. "While I have the highest opinion of your excellent judgment, I believe it is best to leave these matters to the…well, to the experts, of which I am one. As you know, your mother and Ms. de Bourgh have tasked me with the honor of coordinating this wedding. I am humbled and honored that they have such complete faith in my abilities, and I hope that you will too. Therefore, I must politely decline your suggestions and alterations."

At first, Emma thought he was teasing with his formal manner of speech, but the earnest expression on his face told her otherwise.

Without even making eye contact, Mariah responded, "Mr. Collins, you are in luck! Emma here is one of the bridesmaids, and she will be thrilled to help you firm up the seating arrangements this morning. Now, if you both will excuse me, I have some guests to attend to." She gave Emma a weak smile and disappeared into the crowd.

Emma looked down at Mr. Collins. In her heels, she stood a good couple of inches taller than him, and again she resisted the urge to adjust his toupee. Mr. Collins, for his part, looked relieved at not having to deal with Mariah any further.

"Ah, Miss Austen, allow me to introduce myself—"

Emma cut him off. "Oh yes, Mr. Collins, nice to meet you. Mariah has already explained that you are the wedding planner."

He continued on as if Emma had not spoken at all. "I am William Collins, of the Hunsford Design Agency, wedding coordinator and event designer."

Emma was quite sure he puffed out his chest at this declaration.

He went on. "I have been honored by both Ms. de Bourgh and Mrs. Bertram to oversee this momentous event in their lives. As you have no doubt met Ms. de Bourgh, you know how particular she is and what an honor it is to have been chosen among the many other designers she could have picked. I would be most delighted if I could solicit your assistance in the seating arrangements for the rehearsal dinner, specifically. Since we will have the bridesmaids and groomsmen together for the rehearsal, I thought it best to seat them accordingly. If I could just have you look over the names and arrange the pairings, I would be most humbled by your help."

He was so earnest and serious that it took all Emma's self-control not to laugh out loud. She suppressed her smile and took the piece of paper from him.

A waiter came up holding a platter of what looked to be little sweet potato appetizers. Emma politely declined, but she watched as Mr. Collins delicately picked up the bite-sized morsel and studied it as if it were a work of art. He took a bite, and a look of sheer bliss passed over his face. He closed his eyes, savoring every morsel as he chewed, tiny crumbs falling into his mustache.

"What a most exquisite-tasting hors d'oeuvre," he said with complete contentment, popping several more of them in his mouth like they were popcorn.

Emma tried to hide her amusement. He was the most ridiculous man she had ever met, and she fought the urge to wipe the crumbs from his mustache. She forced herself to look away and focus on the paper he had presented to her.

She looked down the list of names and recalled each gentleman she had met over the past few days. The first one was easy. George Wickham. She would definitely pair him with Elizabeth. She had seen the way Elizabeth looked at him at breakfast, and when she came back from golfing that day, she was positively glowing.

JW she would pair with Elinor. God knows Elinor needed to lighten up, and JW's lighthearted and easy manner would help.

Number three on the list was William Elliot. Coincidentally, she looked up and saw Anne talking and laughing with him now. Perfect! That would help keep Frederick away as well.

That left only Frank Churchill and John Thorpe. She hesitated for just a minute on Thorpe's name. She certainly didn't want to be paired with him, and Frank was much better company. She felt just a little guilty as she wrote her own name next to Frank Churchill's.

It was unfortunate that Catherine would have to be paired with John Thorpe. But she figured, of all her sisters, Catherine was the least likely to complain.

With the list completed, she handed it back to Mr. Collins, who thanked her profusely, and as he walked off, she watched his toupee slide even farther down his head.

CHAPTER 19

Anne

"...and the more I saw, the more I found to admire."

- PERSUASION

Anne felt just a little tinge of guilt that she and Elizabeth had left poor Elinor with the horrible reverend and his pretentious wife, but she didn't feel guilty enough to stay. She took the opportunity to look around the crowded balcony. She was pleased to spot Mrs. Croft among the guests. Mrs. Croft caught her eye and made her way toward them, her face beaming with such a friendly smile that Anne could not help but to grin back. She felt a rush of friendship for the motherly woman who had shown her such kindness.

She was surprised when Mrs. Croft stopped and addressed her directly. "Anne, dear, I was hoping we would see you here today! I was telling the admiral about our conversation yesterday. Would you care to join us in our box suite?"

Taken aback, but pleased, Anne replied, "Of course,

Mrs. Croft. I would enjoy that very much."

"Oh, don't be so formal. Please call me Sophie," she said, reaching over and taking Anne's hand in hers. "Come then, let me introduce you to the admiral."

Anne looked worriedly to Elizabeth. "Are you okay if I leave you for a bit, Lizzy?"

"Oh, of course," Elizabeth assured her sister. "Anyway, I think I'm going to see if I can find Wick," she added as she glanced around the room.

When Anne and Sophie reached the Crofts' suite, Anne saw that it was crowded with many of the guests from Mansfield. She normally would have felt out of place among such accomplished society, but Mrs. Croft had a way of easing Anne's anxiety and making her feel welcome and esteemed.

Mrs. Croft introduced her to her husband. Senator Croft had a dignified air that commanded attention. Yet his gentle smile and compassionate eyes gave him a warm and inviting manner, which put Anne even more at ease. Like his wife, he was gregarious and unpretentious.

Anne kept herself well-informed on political issues, and it thrilled her that she could keep up in conversation and debate with the Crofts. She could see why the senator was so successful in politics. He had a way of listening that made you feel like you and he were the only two in the room. When they had exhausted the topic of politics, Anne switched the conversation to something more casual.

"Will you be placing any bets on the horses today?" she asked him in an amused tone.

He smiled over toward his wife. "We never place our bets at the window. We have a standing tradition of just betting between ourselves. What do you say, Sophie darling? Fifty dollars on this next race?" he asked with a teasing grin.

"Too rich for my blood, love, but I'll take your bet for twenty dollars," she said, giving him her radiant smile.

He let out a boisterous laugh in response. "Done!"

Sophie Croft leaned toward Anne and whispered, "I should have taken his fifty dollars; he always bets on the underdog, and he always loses!"

Senator Croft overheard her and pulled his wife in closer to him. "Underdogs have a way of surprising you, my love. Just look at me!" And he gave Anne a small wink and kissed his wife on the forehead.

Anne felt a warmth of feeling for both of them. She marveled at how they complemented each other so perfectly, and she felt a longing for that type of love.

Mrs. Croft looked over Anne's shoulder and nudged her. "I think you have an admirer," she said coyly. "Come along, dear," she said, taking her husband by the arm. "Let's see how much more of your money I can take home today." They both gave Anne an affectionate wave and walked off.

Anne looked over and caught sight of Will Elliot, the handsome, well dressed man she had met upon arriving at the resort. She felt a wave of gratitude to Emma for bringing them outfits today. Normally, she would have been painfully aware of every flaw in her appearance. But now, draped in the flattering dress, she blended seamlessly into the crowd. She looked like she belonged here, and for the fist time since arriving, she almost believed she did.

Will, too, had joined in the festivities and dressed in colorful light blue chinos and a bright pink shirt. Anne thought on anyone else it would look ridiculous, but he managed to pull it off, and she had to admit he looked even more handsome.

Will smiled over his drink and approached her. He had his betting sheet out. "I couldn't help but overhear your conversation with Senator Croft. So, what do you think? Want to help me pick a winner?" His charming smile disarmed Anne.

"What, you mean the nephew of the famous Elliot family of Kellynch Farms doesn't know how to pick a horse?" she teased.

Will immediately tensed up; the somber look in his eyes told her she had hit upon a painful subject. "My father never acknowledged me publicly, so I suppose I shouldn't have expected his family to. I've never had a relationship with my uncle, never even met the man."

Anne looked at Will in surprise. "That's...horrible," she said softly.

Will shrugged, "My uncle has made it very clear to me that I am not welcome. I was just the housemaid's son, my father's biggest mistake. You would think, with my father now gone and the fact that he has no children of his own, he might come around to accepting that I am the only family he has left. But no, the old man is stubborn, if nothing else. Anyway, I don't need him or his money. I think I've done alright without him," he said, a small, sad smile on his face.

Anne felt a surge of sympathy for Will. It never failed to amaze her how even in today's world, there was still so much prejudice and narrow-mindedness.

"Anyway, back to our task at hand. Let's pick a winner," he said, his good humor returning. "I was thinking of putting my money on number eight—Vanity. A little bit of a long shot, but I like the looks of him," he said.

Anne made a face and glanced up at him. He laughed, and it was a natural, good-natured laugh.

He said, "Well, I hope you never play poker, because I can tell you disapprove of my choice."

Anne said hesitantly, "Well, I certainly don't wish to dissuade you if you are set on it."

"Why do I feel like there's a 'but' coming?" he teased

her.

"Well, it's just that—look here," she said, pulling out the betting sheet, "it states he's had many injuries in his short career, including a recent leg injury. I don't think he's had enough time to heal."

Will gave her an approving look. "Interesting. Then what are your thoughts on my second choice, Widow's Peak?" He glanced up, looking for a hint in her face.

She looked down at the spotted mare prancing to the gate. "A bit too excitable, I think," Anne said, growing more confident.

"Well, if I may be so bold as to ask, which one would you put your money on?"

Anne looked out at the parade of horses and pointed at a beautiful white stallion. "Right there, Captain of the Seas. He's good on the turf, consistent, and has a long stride. He's ridden by an experienced jockey who handles him well, and he was raised on a farm here in Kentucky. If I were the betting kind, that's where I would put my money."

Will placed his wager at the betting window, adding an extra one for Anne's pick for good measure. When he returned, tickets in hand and two mint juleps perfectly chilled, he offered one to Anne with a grin. "To luck," he toasted, raising his glass. "May both our horses bring us victory."

Anne raised her glass and sipped around the sprig of mint. "Cheers," she said as she eyed him above the rim of her glass.

As the race started, the room seemed to get more crowded, as everyone on the balcony pulled in closer to watch the race. Anne watched with a rising sense of anticipation and a rush of adrenaline. The horses entered the gates and were off.

In all the excitement and cheering, she hadn't realized how close Will had come, and he placed his arm along her back. A warm shiver ran down her spine. She wasn't sure how she felt about this. His attention was flattering and she was genuinely enjoying his company but still she felt hesitation at his nearness.

The yelling inside the box reached a crescendo as the horses crossed the finish line.

"I can't believe it!" Will exclaimed. "Anne, you really are amazing—your horse won! Well, I'll be damned," He shook his head in disbelief.

At that moment, Anne heard a voice from behind them. *That* voice.

"You would be wise to listen to Anne. She has a level head and common sense."

Both she and Will turned around to see Frederick Wentworth standing there.

She wasn't sure when he'd arrived, but he had a smile on his face and seemed relaxed. She immediately felt uncomfortable with how close she was to Will, and she moved slightly out of his reach.

"Freddy," was all she could manage to say.

"Hello, Anne," he said, his gaze now fully meeting hers, unlike the other night.

Will looked from Anne to Frederick. "I take it you two are acquainted," he said with a hint of annoyance in his voice.

Anne did not reply, curious to see how Frederick would respond.

"Yes, Anne and I are old friends," he said, keeping his dark brown eyes on Anne's.

"Are we?" she practically whispered in return.

He was just about to reply when a young woman came up and wrapped her arms around his shoulders.

"So, this is where you disappeared to, Cappy," she said, smiling up at him warmly and giving a little nod to Anne and Will.

Anne immediately recognized her as the woman she

had seen flirting with Frederick the night before, and she cringed at the intimacy of the nickname.

He blushed. "Louisa, this is William Elliot and an old acquaintance of mine from high school, Anne Austen."

Louisa seemed friendly enough, and she immediately launched into pleasant conversation, but Anne could no longer focus. To Will, Frederick had referred to her as a friend. But now, in front of Louisa, she had been relegated to an old acquaintance. Anne felt her spirits sink again.

As Louisa chatted on, Anne looked up to see that Mrs. Croft had approached her once again. Frederick saw her coming as well, and he looked up at her eagerly.

"Oh, Sophie, how wonderful to see you here! Is Tom here, too?"

Anne was struck by his lack of formality with the Crofts. Mrs. Croft did not seem fazed at all as she turned to him.

"Yes, he's over there. But you can talk business later. Let's enjoy the afternoon, shall we? Captain, I'm delighted to see you've already met Anne. This is the young lady I was telling you about yesterday. I would like to see what we can do to help support her literacy program." She beamed at Anne.

Frederick appeared as confused as Anne felt.

Flustered, Frederick responded, "I had no idea when you were speaking to me yesterday that it was Anne you were referring to. Anne was a friend in high school; we are well acquainted."

Anne cringed at the word "acquainted." There was that awful word again.

Mrs. Croft seemed to process this information with a contemplative look. Then, she turned and smiled at Anne. "We've just brought the captain on to help with Tom's gubernatorial campaign. We're excited to have him, and since you already know each other, I'm sure he will be able to help your library's program get some visibility."

Anne looked up and caught Frederick's eye. He was blushing, and she was sure she was too, based on the heat in her cheeks. Mrs. Croft appeared to notice their embarrassment but did not comment.

Anne recovered her composure and turned to Frederick. "Congratulations. I'm sure this is going to be an exciting position for you, and well-deserved."

Frederick also seemed to recover a little of his equilibrium. He looked admiringly at Mrs. Croft. "I'm thrilled to be working with the Senator and his wife. You won't find two better people in politics."

Louisa appeared to be bored by this point, and she tugged on his sleeve and pulled him away. "You heard Mrs. Croft, Freddy; let's save the politics for another time. Today is about fun. Let's go put our bets in for the next race."

He turned to follow Louisa and gave Anne one last look. "It was great to see you again, Annie." And then he was gone.

CHAPTER 20

Elizabeth

"There is a stubbornness about me that never can bear to be frightened at the will of others.

My courage always rises with every attempt to intimidate me."

\- PRIDE AND PREJUDICE

Elizabeth glanced around the crowded balcony with an eye out for Wickham but was pleasantly surprised when she spotted her cousin. Fanny was looking a bit lost among the crowd and immediately brightened upon seeing Elizabeth.

"Oh my gosh, don't you look beautiful!" Fanny gushed. "I wish I were brave enough to wear a hat. I just always feel like my head is too small and the hat swallows me up," she said good-naturedly. "I was looking for Edmund, but I think he may have been swept away by his groomsmen. I'm sure they whisked him off to place some bets or get some drinks."

Elizabeth thought she detected a little resignation in

her cousin's voice. "They do seem like a rowdy bunch when they get together," she offered in agreement.

Fanny shook her head sadly. "I know they are Edmund's closest friends from his college days, but they are the worst influence. I would never say anything bad about them to Edmund, but they get into all kinds of trouble. There's too much drinking and gambling when they're around, especially JW and Wickham. That's why I was hoping Darcy or Knightley might be here. They can usually keep Edmund more sensible than those guys," Fanny said, a little despondently.

Elizabeth's head popped up at the mention of Darcy. "Oh, I didn't realize Darcy and Edmund were such good friends." She hoped she sounded nonchalant and only casually interested.

Fanny beamed. "Oh yes. Have you met him yet? I just adore Darcy. He's such a sweetheart, and he would do anything for his friends. Honestly, I can't figure it out. He never has a girlfriend, yet he's so kind, and obviously good-looking." At this, she blushed.

Elizabeth trusted Fanny's judgment, and she knew her cousin's high opinion was hard won, but she couldn't reconcile this version of Darcy with the one from her date and, certainly, not with the one from Wickham's tale.

Fanny continued, "Funny story, but I encouraged Darcy to use Emma's dating app. When she reached out to me and Edmund asking if we had any friends we could get to sign up, I immediately thought of Darcy." She gave a little giggle. "And he actually did it! He signed up and went on a date. I felt so bad that it didn't work out. I think he really found her interesting, but he got the impression he wasn't her type. He's so shy around women, and it's a shame, because he's the absolute sweetest guy."

Elizabeth felt stunned. Darcy had liked her? Had her own feelings been that transparent? Had he just been trying to avoid being dumped? Her mind was a whirlwind of thoughts.

"Anyway, since you're by yourself, why don't you come with me and I'll show you around some of the suites? The views from the upper balconies are amazing," Fanny offered.

Elizabeth agreed and followed behind her. She was still trying to process her thoughts around Darcy when she looked up to find him coming toward them.

Dressed in a long black coat and tails, he stood out among all the colorful suits and ties. As he approached, his tailcoat flowed gracefully behind him. The top hat perched upon his head perfectly complemented his dashing appearance. Elizabeth thought he looked breathtakingly handsome—with the exception of that stupid scowl he always seemed to be wearing.

"Darcy! We were just talking about you," Fanny said as she beamed up at him.

He came forward and gave her a huge hug. "And how is the beautiful bride-to-be today?" he asked with a smile that lit up his whole face.

Elizabeth felt a stab of jealousy at his obvious affection for Fanny.

Fanny started to answer when she spotted Edmund. "Better now," she said, her face bright with happiness. "Darcy, do you mind showing Lizzy around one of the suites? I promised her a tour, but I'm going to try to catch up with Edmund. Lizzy, are you fine hanging out with Darcy for a while?"

Fanny headed off before she could respond, and Elizabeth had a sneaking suspicion that it was no accident she was leaving her with Darcy.

Elizabeth looked up at him. His smile had all but disappeared. After their last conversation, she felt awkward and uncomfortable. Judging by his nervous posture, she assumed he felt the same way.

She tried to regain a little of her composure and smiled up at him. "I see someone got into the spirit of the day," she said, hoping her lighthearted approach would break the ice.

He looked at her deadpan and said, "What, this old thing?"

Elizabeth let out a real, genuine, boisterous laugh. "Oh my god, Darcy! Did you just make a joke?" she asked, teasingly.

He gave her a huge smile, even bigger than the one he had given to Fanny, and Elizabeth felt her heart start to beat wildly. What the hell was happening!? This was Darcy!

He cleared his throat and asked her, "If you'd like, I can show you our box suite?"

She looked around and, having lost sight of her sisters, figured she might as well take Darcy up on the offer. As she followed him, he turned back with a mischievous smile. "Just a heads-up—my aunt is here. I'm assuming you're okay with meeting Miranda Priestly?"

"Two jokes in two minutes! Darcy, be still my heart," she said, pleased he had remembered their conversation from that first date.

But as they approached the suite, Elizabeth felt butterflies in her stomach at the prospect of meeting Catherine de Bourgh in person.

When she stepped into the suite, its opulence struck her right away. Large floor-to-ceiling windows offered a panoramic view of the track, and all along the wall ran a fully stocked bar with a tuxedoed bartender standing at attention. Elizabeth cringed as she heard her heels squeak across the marble floors.

The only person in the suite other than the bartender was an elderly woman staring out onto the track through a pair of binoculars. Elizabeth understood immediately the comparisons to the fictional Miranda Priestly. Her demeanor alone was imposing and intimidating. She had a classic bob, large sunglasses, a long blue dress, and black knee-high boots. It was a look befitting a woman much younger than sixty-five, yet Catherine de Bourgh pulled it off.

Darcy approached her and as he leaned over, she jutted out her chin to receive a quick kiss on the cheek.

"Good morning, Aunt Cathy!" he said cheerfully.

His aunt remained looking straight ahead through her binoculars. "Darcy, you know how I loathe nicknames." Her voice was sharp and curt. Elizabeth could easily imagine how intimidating that voice would be barking out orders.

Darcy smiled and stepped back to introduce Elizabeth. "Aunt Catherine, I want to introduce you to Elizabeth Austen."

Elizabeth leaned forward, offering a hand to shake. "Lovely to meet you, and, please, call me Lizzy."

She heard Darcy give a choked little cough and noticed a smile at the corners of his mouth.

His aunt lowered the binoculars and turned to take in the full sight of Elizabeth. She ignored Elizabeth's hand, and her eyes swept dismissively over her pantsuit, a look of sharp disapproval evident on her face.

"Hmph, are you wearing pants? I thought there was a dress code. I guess I was mistaken," she said and sniffed. "It's your first time in a box suite." She looked pointedly at Elizabeth.

"Oh yes, I—" Elizabeth started to answer, but Ms. de Bourgh cut her off.

"It wasn't a question, merely an observation. Perhaps next time you will know how to dress appropriately." Ms. de Bourgh gave her another appraising look. "Although I do like the hat," she said begrudgingly. Then she turned to continue staring out over the track.

A moment later, she said, "Darcy, be a dear and ask the bartender to fix me a bourbon and water."

Elizabeth noticed that the bartender heard every word and started making the drink even before Darcy walked over.

"Elizabeth, tell me how it is exactly that you know my nephew?" she asked, and she turned to face Elizabeth and give her full attention.

Elizabeth glanced over at Darcy, but he was now engaged in conversation with the bartender, who seemed happy to have someone other than Ms. de Bourgh to chat with. She was sure he would not want to explain that they met on a dating app, so instead she replied, "We both work in publishing."

Ms. de Bourgh arched an eyebrow, which made her appear even more intimidating. "Surely you don't work at Pemberley," she said, more a statement than a question.

Elizabeth refused to be insulted. "No, I work at Charlotte Lucas."

Ms. de Bourgh scoffed loudly. "Charlotte Lucas? My god, they're still in business? They print rubbish! You would never see the pages of Pemberley polluted with that type of trash."

Oddly, Elizabeth couldn't bring herself to feel insulted. Catherine's over-the-top haughtiness struck her as ridiculous, which made it easy to relax and give little weight to her words.

"We're actually the fourth largest publisher in Indianapolis and climbing, thanks to Bookstagram and BookTok raising the popularity of romantic fiction," Elizabeth replied coolly.

"You're pretty confident for someone who won't have a job for long. Charlotte Lucas Publishing has no money and even fewer prospects. You'll be back to burdening your parents in no time," she said with no attempt to hide her scorn.

"I have no parents," Elizabeth replied tersely. She forced herself to maintain eye contact.

If she'd expected her orphan status to melt Ms. de Bourgh's cold exterior, she was mistaken. The woman showed no emotion and returned to looking through her binoculars.

Darcy returned with his aunt's drink. She lowered her binoculars, took a sip, and made a face. "You'd think we could at least get a decent drink up here."

"Would you like something else, Aunt Catherine?" Darcy asked without an ounce of impatience. Elizabeth marveled at how little his aunt's demeanor fazed him.

"There's no point. It will taste just as awful!" she said and waved him off. "No, I'll just have to make do with this. And Darcy, where is Caroline? I expected you to bring her up here today. I wanted to congratulate her on her book sales. Of course, when I write *my* memoir, I'm sure it will rival hers, if not surpass it entirely. After all, my life has been far more interesting."

"I'm sure she would be delighted to hear your thoughts on her success, but as you well know, Aunt Catherine, Caroline had prior engagements," Darcy replied, obviously a little uncomfortable at the reference to Caroline.

"What a shame. The company up here has been so dull today," she said, and with that she turned her binoculars back to the track. They had been summarily dismissed.

Well, the devil may not be wearing Prada, but she's certainly wearing a blue dress, Elizabeth mused to herself.

CHAPTER 21

Catherine

"Where the heart is really attached,

*I know very well how little one can be pleased with the
attention of anybody else."*

- NORTHANGER ABBEY

Catherine once again found herself alone in the crowd.
She couldn't help but wish Henry was here. But he
was working at the resort today, and, of course, he would
not have been on the guest list, she reminded herself.
Her sisters had all managed to find themselves drawn into
conversations, but Catherine felt the familiar feeling of
self-consciousness come over her. She had little interest in
the races. She thought it was cruel to the horses, and she
couldn't bear to watch.

She looked around for an open seat, pulled out her
book, and sat down, hoping to go unnoticed. After a few
minutes, though, she became aware of someone looking
over at her and realized it was John Thorpe. She steeled
herself and gave a polite smile as he made his way over.

John had embraced a more casual look today, dressed

in khakis and a blazer over a pink dress shirt with no tie. He wasn't too bad looking when he cleaned himself up, and when he was sober. He smiled graciously at her.

"Well, look at us—we match today! What are you reading?" he asked, sitting in the chair beside her. He reached over and pulled the book toward him. "*Twilight!* I've seen it. Stupid movie," he said, dismissively.

Catherine wished he would leave, but when he didn't, she felt she had to keep the conversation going. "What do you like to read, John?" she asked, trying to sound even a little interested.

"Read? I don't touch books. Too boring," he said scornfully. "Even in college I paid someone to read them for me so I could graduate." He had a sense of pride that made Catherine's blood boil. "Ever been to the races before?" he asked her. It was clear he'd changed the subject to one he felt more comfortable with.

Despite the fact that she had grown up in Kentucky, she'd never been to a racetrack. "No, this is my first time," she replied, wishing with all her heart that he would just go away.

Thorpe's face lit up as he said, "Well, aren't you lucky to have me as your escort? I know all about horses. Own several myself. I'll teach you everything you need to know. For starters, we need a drink, and I know just the one for you!" Before she could interject, Catherine found herself being swept away, arm in arm with John Thorpe.

He ordered them mint juleps and took her down close to the field, right up against the racetrack. Catherine took one sip of her drink and almost immediately spat it out.

"Oh my god, that's absolutely terrible!" she gasped.

Thorpe looked offended. "That right there is summertime in a glass, refreshing and minty. What's not to like?" he asked, taking another large drink from his glass.

"Is there alcohol in it?" she sputtered, her face still

scrunched up from the distasteful swig.

He laughed and said, "Of course there is; what's the point, otherwise! That's Kentucky bourbon. Don't worry, darling, keep drinking it. It will grow on you." Thorpe then proceeded to down his own drink.

For once, Thorpe hadn't been exaggerating—he really did know a lot about horses. He explained everything from their jockeys to the stables they were groomed in to their winning streaks and purses. At first, Catherine feigned interest and listened with undivided attention. But as Thorpe consumed more drinks, he became louder and more boisterous. He finally resorted to skipping the mint julep and just having them bring him straight bourbon.

He started heckling the jockeys as they paraded their horses to the track. It was obvious he found himself amusing, but Catherine became more uncomfortable and embarrassed. She was soon bored of listening to him rattle on, and she looked around, hoping to catch sight of her sisters and have an excuse to leave.

For his part, Thorpe seemed oblivious to her disinterest. "So, what do you think of your day at the races, Barbie?" he asked, leaning in a little too close for her comfort, and she cringed at his nickname for her but did not correct him.

"I'd much rather be reading a book," she said, not out of rudeness but as a statement of fact.

Thorpe gave her a sideways look and started to laugh. "Read a book? Yeah right, you're funny," he snorted.

The day dragged on, and Catherine thought it would never end. When Elinor's text finally came through that they were ready to go and wondering where she was, she was relieved. She hurriedly thanked Thorpe for the afternoon and ran off before he could insist she stay.

CHAPTER 22

Elizabeth

*"She had a lively, playful disposition that delighted in
anything ridiculous."*

- PRIDE AND PREJUDICE

The day at the races had left Elizabeth struggling
to make sense of her afternoon with Darcy. If she
was being honest with herself, she had actually enjoyed
the day and would even go so far as to say it had been
fun. Darcy had seemed more at ease, their conversation
relaxed and easy. Between work and books, they found
they had much in common. Granted, his aunt's behavior
had been horrible. But that wasn't his fault, and he had
seemed genuinely embarrassed about the way she'd
treated Elizabeth.

A feeling of restlessness had overcome her, and now
that they were back at the resort, she was itching to do
something. A text from Fanny came through with perfect
timing.

She asked her sisters hopefully, "Did you see Fanny's
invite to meet her and Edmund down at the Pump Room

for drinks and karaoke?" Downing a few beers and eating some incredibly unhealthy appetizers sounded like just what she needed.

"I'm in as long as you promise not to sing," Emma said, her eyes gleaming with humor.

Elizabeth let out a giggle. "I'm not making any promises. Who knows what could happen after a few drinks!" she said playfully.

Out of all the sisters, only Emma could hold a tune, and she definitely liked to flaunt this fact over her sisters' heads. But Elizabeth had no qualms about getting on stage and singing, and if it embarrassed her sister, that made it even more fun.

Catherine, already in her pajamas, had curled up into the couch and was contently buried in her book. She pried her eyes away from it and gave her sisters a pleading look. "I'm all peopled out today. I just got comfortable, and I've been longing to have some reading time. Will you be terribly upset if I don't join you? Besides, I've already been to the Pump Room."

Emma looked at her curiously. "You've been there already? With who?" But before Catherine could reply she asked excitedly, "Ooh, do you think I can get some good pics in there?"

Catherine nodded. "I'm sure you will love it, Em. It's a beautiful spot." She offered a small smile before returning to her book.

Elinor also made excuses but disappeared into the other suite before anyone could ask any questions.

Emma turned to Elizabeth with concern. "What's up with her? She's been so moody this whole trip."

Elizabeth agreed. Something was clearly going on with Elinor. It wasn't unusual for her to hold her feelings inside, but it wasn't like her to be so snappy and quiet. Tomorrow, Elizabeth would make it a point to find out what was wrong. But tonight, she needed to get rid of this antsy feeling and go out and have some fun.

"Anne, are you in? We need at least one of you to keep us out of trouble," Elizabeth pleaded. Anne could always be counted on to make sure she and Emma didn't get too carried away.

Anne gave a knowing smile. "Count me in. I haven't had any time with Fanny. Hopefully I'll have a chance to catch up with the bride."

***

The atmosphere of the Pump Room immediately put Elizabeth into a good mood. Music and laughter filled the air, and she felt a rush of excitement and energy. It was a unique setting with a spacious garden patio. The lights from the garden illuminated the bar and gave it a cozy feel.

She looked around for Fanny and Edmund and spotted Fanny sitting alone at a large table full of pitchers and mugs of beer. Fanny didn't even drink! Elizabeth felt a pang of sympathy for her cousin.

Fanny jumped up with a look of pleasure spreading across her face. "Yay! You came! But where are Elinor and Catherine?"

Elizabeth explained that they had stayed back, worn out after the day's activities. "What are you doing sitting by yourself?" she asked, looking around for the rest of the party.

Fanny gave a little nod up toward the stage. "Julia and Mariah were just here, but they went to say hello to someone out on the patio. Edmund is up there with Wick, Frank, and JW, picking out songs for karaoke later. Can you believe they've talked Edmund into singing?" she asked, looking a little skeptical.

Elizabeth noticed the stage for the first time. It was

dimly lit with a microphone stand and a large screen that displayed song lyrics. Off to the side of the stage, there was a grand piano. Edmund and his groomsmen were loud and boisterous as they scrolled through the musical selections.

"I'm afraid the guys have been drinking for a while now," Fanny said in a raised voice, trying to be heard over the loud music. There was definitely a note of disapproval in her voice, and Elizabeth suspected she was not too pleased that Edmund had been pulled away by his college pals. "And, as you can see, there is plenty to drink," she added, sweeping her hand over the mugs and pitchers on the table.

Emma gave a look of disapproval. "Sorry, Fan, but I don't do beer. I'm going to grab a chardonnay from the bar."

Elizabeth let out a laugh and pulled over a mug and pitcher. "You are such a snob, Emma," she said teasingly, trying to make light of their earlier conversations.

Emma scoffed. "Pretty rich coming from you, Lizzy." But she, too, gave her sister a smile as she headed toward the bar.

Anne took a seat next to Fanny and started to pour herself a mug as well. "Can I pour you a glass?" She asked her cousin

Fanny gave Anne a tired smile. "I don't drink but thank you. I'll just stick to water."

Elizabeth took in the sight of her cousin. She looked so young and out of her element here in the raucous bar. Fanny was the same age as Emma, but Elizabeth couldn't help but think how very different the two cousins were.

Julia returned to the table, without Mariah and visibly upset. Elizabeth looked up to see that the gentleman the two sisters had been speaking to was now leaning into and kissing Mariah.

Anne had noticed too and turned looking surprised

said to Julia, "Oh, how nice. I see Mariah's fiancé was able to make it to the wedding after all."

Julia rolled her eyes and snorted. "As if."

"Wait, Mariah is engaged? And that's not her fiancé?" Elizabeth asked, more than a little confused. She snuck a peek back toward the couple and cringed at their over-the-top display of affection.

Julia's lip quivered and she said angrily, "That is most definitely *not* James Rushworth. That happens to be Henry Crawford—who I thought was interested in me until an hour ago." Her anger quickly turned into tears of frustration. "It's not enough for Mariah to have a fiancé. Apparently, she has to steal any man who shows an interest in me as well."

Elizabeth grew increasingly uncomfortable watching the two of them making out in the back of the pub. "Isn't she concerned that her fiancé will find out?" she couldn't help asking Julia.

Julia shrugged her shoulders. "Who's going to tell?" she replied, picking up her purse and storming off toward the exit.

Elizabeth understood. It was the golden rule of sisterhood: no matter how much sisters hurt each other; they would always hold one another's secrets.

As she watched Julia leave, she caught sight of the arrival of more of Edmund's friends. Among them were Edmund's best man, George Knightley, Jane Fairfax, Caroline Bingley, and Darcy.

At the sight of Darcy, Elizabeth felt her heartbeat quicken. *What the hell is that about?* It was Darcy, for goodness' sake. *You don't even like him*, she reminded herself. Yet, she found her eyes glancing back over to him. He was, as usual, impeccably dressed in a suit, but tonight he wore no tie, and his white-collared shirt was slightly open at the top. She would have said he looked a little more relaxed than usual, but then she caught sight of his signature scowl.

Caroline stunned in a billowing white shirt dress that accented her toned, tanned features. Elizabeth had to admit, they made a striking couple. Darcy caught her eye as they made their way over and gave her a curt nod. They pulled some chairs up to the table so they would all fit, and Elizabeth found herself sitting next to both Darcy and Caroline.

Caroline eyed the pitchers of beer with the same look of disapproval Emma had. "Beer? Really? Oh, good lord, Darcy, where have you dragged me to?" she said, letting out a sigh and sneering.

Darcy looked nonplussed. "It's a brewery, Caroline, and I was under the impression *you* dragged me here."

Caroline rolled her eyes indignantly.

Elizabeth let out a little giggle. She was starting to appreciate Darcy's droll sense of humor. She glanced at him and thought she saw the faintest hint of a smile on his lips.

"Do you plan to sing for us tonight, Darcy?" Elizabeth asked him teasingly, hoping the rapport they'd built up over the afternoon would reappear.

He seemed to recognize her teasing tone and shook his head. "No. Trust me, Elizabeth, you do not want to hear me sing. I've been told I sound like a dying goose. You only want me up there if your aim is to clear the room."

She let out another laugh, and when she smiled up at Darcy she was immediately rewarded with a shy smile in return.

Caroline chimed in, "Darcy can't stand to be embarrassed. He would never allow such humiliation. And I don't understand the obsession with bad singing. It's so painful to listen to. I really can't stand when people with no talent get up there and make fools of themselves."

"What a shame," said Elizabeth. "You're missing out

on all the fun. And I do love to have fun."

"Did I hear someone say they like to have fun?"

Elizabeth looked up to see that Wickham had made his way over from the stage and was leaning across the table to grab a pitcher and a mug of beer. He was beaming down at Elizabeth and purposely avoiding eye contact with Darcy.

When he'd poured his drink and taken a sip, he held out his hand to her. "Would you care to come to the dance floor with me, love?" he said.

"I sure hope you dance better than you golf," she teased, and she felt her pulse pound as he took her hand in his. She glanced back toward Darcy, but he didn't look up or acknowledge Wickham. Together, they walked toward the dance floor.

Wickham pulled her in close and whispered into her ear, "For the record, I do a lot of things better than I golf," he said, and the boyish smile was now a wicked grin. He pressed his arm around her back and took her other hand in his. Her heart continued to beat with anticipation.

"So, tell me, George—"

"Call me Wick, love. All my friends do." He leaned toward her and, for a brief second, she thought he was going to kiss her. Instead, he whispered into her ear, "Because no one can hold a candle to me." He winked and once again smiled his wolfish grin.

She had to stifle a laugh. Did that line really work on women?

As they danced, she noticed that Wickham was a little unsteady on his feet, and she suspected he was getting pretty drunk. Elizabeth thought about Fanny's words from earlier and her dislike of Edmund's friends, who she had complained were too fond of drinking and gambling. Wickham's hand moved farther down her back, and he tugged her in closer to him.

Elizabeth felt increasingly uncomfortable. She didn't

want to lead him on, especially if he'd been drinking. She moved away, putting a little more space between them.

"How about a little nightcap back at my suite?" he asked. His breath was heavy in Elizabeth's ear, the smell causing her to turn her head.

"Not going to happen, Wick." She gave a forced giggle, trying to sound carefree and casual to mask how uncomfortable he was making her feel.

He took a step back and frowned down at her. "Suit yourself, love. You don't know what you're missing." He shrugged, but the anger in his voice caught her off guard.

Still, Elizabeth was willing to give him the benefit of doubt. It was obvious he'd had too much to drink tonight, but his sulkiness at her refusal left her feeling a bit uneasy.

She let her eyes wander back to the table, looking for Darcy, and she felt a pang of disappointment when she saw his seat was empty. He and Caroline were gone.

CHAPTER 23

Emma

"Why she did not like Jane Fairfax might be a difficult question to answer..."

- EMMA

Emma was pleased to see George Knightley had arrived. He was always pleasant company, but she couldn't help but feel a stab of jealousy to see he was with Jane Fairfax again. Emma gave them a welcoming smile and wasn't surprised when Jane gave her just a slight nod of acknowledgment in return. Emma felt the sting of embarrassment from having insulted Jane's aunt earlier. Apparently, Jane was going to hold a grudge.

She tried to figure out what it was about Jane that bothered her so much. She didn't have the sophistication or money of Caroline or Julia, yet she carried herself with an air of haughtiness that just got under Emma's skin. Watching her with George, Emma felt certain they weren't together. Knightley was friendly and accommodating with her, but he was that way with everyone. Jane, for her part, seemed aloof and quiet.

The music came to an abrupt stop, and the DJ's voice boomed over the crowd announcing it was time for karaoke.

The chords to Garth Brooks' "Friends in Low Places" rang out across the room, and Emma looked up to see JW taking the mic. With his Southern drawl, he belted out the first verse. The bar sent up a raucous round of applause, and before long, JW had the whole bar singing along to the chorus.

Frank Churchill took the stage next. "For this one, folks, I'm going to need a partner," he said, his voice charming and playful. He put his hand up over his brows, and his eyes swept over the room. Emma thought she saw Jane start to edge forward. Was she actually going to go up there? But Frank Churchill's gaze had landed squarely on Emma.

He crooked his finger, urging her forward. "Emma, care to join me on stage?" Thrilled to be singled out, she handed her phone to Anne. "Can you record this for me!? It's going to make for great content!" Anne sighed dutifully and took the phone.

Emma pushed her long blond locks behind her ears, adjusted the hem of her skirt, and made a point to brush past Jane on her way up to the stage.

Frank looked surprised that she'd taken him up on it. But Emma thrived in the spotlight. She clutched her microphone and looked to the screen, ready for lyrics. When the music to "Summer Nights" from *Grease* rang out, Frank playfully leaned in and hammed up his best John Travolta impression.

Emma took her cue and played right along. Her vocals sounded amazing and caught the attention of the room. Their playful and flirtatious dance moves rallied the crowd, who quickly joined in clapping and singing.

As the song drew to a close, a wave of smug satisfaction

washed over her. She had nailed it, and she knew it. Frank made a great partner too; their energy and chemistry on stage had been undeniable. Although she wasn't looking to start something with him, right now she could have hugged him for giving her some great content. She couldn't wait to share this with her followers.

Breathless and energized, she returned to the table. George Knightley gave her an approving smile.

"I had no idea you could sing so well," he said, admiration clear in his voice. For some reason, his words meant more to her than all the applause. Knightley's approval was never easily earned, and knowing he didn't find her performance silly or frivolous filled her with satisfaction. He had genuinely appreciated her talent, and that realization thrilled her more than she expected.

She looked up, surprised to see that Frank had returned to the microphone. She wondered if he was going to ask her to do another song, but instead he said, "Ladies and gentlemen, we have a rare treat for you tonight. We have the lovely and talented Miss Jane Fairfax here in the audience, and I would like to invite her up here to play a song for y'all." He looked at Jane and, just as he had with Emma, motioned her up to the stage.

Jane looked around hesitantly, and Emma was dismayed to see that Knightley gave her the same smile of approval he'd given her earlier. "Please, Jane, it would be a treat to hear you play for us tonight."

This seemed to be the encouragement Jane needed, for she shyly stood up and took the stage. But instead of walking to the microphone, she sat down at the piano next to the stage. It was as if the piano transformed the shy, demure girl into a woman full of confidence and self-assuredness.

She ran her fingers over the keys. A melody sounded, and Jane's soulful voice sang out, "Mmm, mmm, mmm." She closed her eyes and belted out a fiery rendition of "If

I Ain't Got You" by Alicia Keys.

The room went still, mesmerized by the sheer emotion in her voice.

Emma could see that Jane was drawing in the crowd with every note. Elizabeth and Anne were completely transfixed. Knightley showed the same expression of admiration that minutes before had been showered on Emma. She looked up to see Frank's reaction. He was looking on in admiration too, but she thought there was also a hint of sadness in his eyes.

Emma tried to push down the wave of jealousy and resentment. It was silly of her to care that Jane was so talented, but somehow she felt it took away from her own performance.

Jane returned to the table, radiantly blushing and seeming embarrassed by everyone's profusive praise. Emma had hoped she would come back bragging or gloating so she wouldn't feel so guilty about her own resentment.

But Jane's humbleness only made Emma dislike her even more.

CHAPTER 24

Anne

"We certainly do not forget you, so soon as you forget us. It is, perhaps, our fate rather than our merit. We cannot help ourselves."

- PERSUASION

There is only so much karaoke a person can take—especially a sober one, thought Anne. She had enjoyed watching Emma and Frank, and the performance by Jane had left her in tears, but now she was over it.

Fanny, too, looked like she had had enough. But Edmund and his friends had returned to the table, and it was clear they had no intention of calling it a night. To Anne's dismay, they ordered another round of drinks.

Wickham nudged Fanny. "Come on, love; I think it's your turn at the mic," he said, giving Fanny a lighthearted nudge.

"Me?" cried Fanny, looking absolutely panicked. "But I can't sing at all, and I have terrible stage fright."

"Oh, c'mon, darling, no excuses. Bertram, get the

little missus up there."

Fanny looked to Edmund with terror in her eyes, hoping for support. Anne was pleased to see that he immediately came to Fanny's defense.

"Lay off, Wick. She said she's not interested," Edmund said, his voice carrying a hint of anger.

Wickham backed off. "It was all in good fun, no harm intended," he said. He grabbed his beer, polished it off in one long gulp, and wiped his hand across his mouth. "But you're not off the hook, Bertram. Now, get your ass up there and pick a song."

Edmund leaned over and gave Fanny a kiss. "Just a few more, babe," he said and hurried off to catch up to Wickham, who was headed toward the stage.

Anne looked over to see her sisters in lively conversations. She let out a sigh.

Fanny gave her a sympathetic smile. "Shall we go sit out on the patio for a while? It's less stuffy out there, and a little less noisy."

Anne readily agreed, and they stepped out into the cooler evening air.

"So, how are you feeling about the big day?" Anne asked her cousin with genuine interest. Despite Fanny's young age, Anne thought she carried herself with an air of maturity.

"I know what people think," Fanny said, eyeing Anne with a wry smile. "I know they think I'm much too young to be getting married, or that I don't know what I'm getting myself into." She paused and looked out toward the gardens. Anne followed her gaze and took in the lights sparkling off the trees.

"I've loved him for so long, Anne," she said, sounding confident and happy. "I don't have a single doubt in my mind. He loved me when I felt no one else did. Those years after my mom passed were so lonely. I was so grateful to have you and your sisters for those short few weeks each summer. But then you'd all leave, and things would go back to normal, and it would be worse than before. Until Edmund came along. His friendship helped me, and then his love saved me." Anne felt her heart ache for her cousin. She had just described her own feelings toward Frederick.

"You know I almost lost him?" she continued softly, her eyes welling up with tears. "He met someone the year he went to Oxford. We still texted and kept in touch over the phone. He would call all excited about this girl he had met—Mary. I don't think he had any idea that I was already in love with him at that point. When he started dating her, I decided it might be time for me to date as well. I went out a few times with one of Edmund's friends. I thought he tried to get too serious too soon, but I know now that my reluctance was simply because he wasn't Edmund." She let out a little ironic laugh. "He's actually here tonight. He's the one hitting on Mariah despite the huge rock on her finger, so, yeah, dodged a bullet there. Anyway, Edmund dated Mary the whole year he was gone, but I think he started to suspect she was only after his money."

Fanny turned to Anne now, her expressive face so full of sadness. "Why are men so stupid?" Surprised at her cousin's frankness, Anne burst into laughter, and Fanny giggled along with her.

Fanny said with a satisfied air, "I mean, it was so obvious to me that she was after his money! But he had to figure it out on his own, and thankfully he did. Edmund came back and immediately proposed to me. He said he already had what he was looking for; he just needed to be without it for a while to realize it."

Anne felt a rush of emotions listening to Fanny's story, her heart tightening with a familiar ache. In so many ways, it mirrored her own feelings about Frederick. "I don't think a woman ever really gets over her first love,"

Anne lamented with a sigh. "It's a hole that no one else ever fills, no matter how much time passes. Every new face, every new prospect-you can't help but measure them against *him*." She swallowed hard, trying to keep her emotions in check. "And yet, men seem able to move on so effortlessly, while we are stuck in the same lonely place."

She leaned over and gave Fanny a hug. "Anyway, you're lucky he found his way back to you. I'm so happy for you."

Anne was startled by a chair scraping the floor, and she saw that someone had been sitting at one of the patio tables nearby. She glanced up and froze as she realized it was Freddy. Had he overheard their conversation? With all the noise from the music and the crowd inside, she doubted it. Plus, she and Fanny hadn't been speaking that loud. No, he couldn't possibly have overheard. Still, her heart was practically beating out of her chest as he walked toward them. She took a quick inhalation of breath.

"Anne, I was wondering if I might have a moment?" he said, his eyes locking on hers. Fanny gave Anne a hint of a smile and quickly excused herself to go check on Edmund. Suddenly, Anne found herself alone with Frederick for the first time in seven years.

"You look well, Anne," he said, more relaxed than he'd been on previous occasions. Anne cringed at his words. *Well.* Not pretty, not better, not good…just, well.

He however, looked far better than just *well.* He was confident and mature and yet beneath it all, there was still something boyish about him, something that made her heart ache with memory.

"You look great, Freddy," she managed to say. She blushed when she used the old familiar nickname. "I'm sorry; I know everyone calls you 'Captain' now, but old habits are hard to break." She averted her eyes to avoid his penetrating stare. But he moved in closer and lifted her chin up toward his face.

She fought against the emotions threatening to break free, but as her gaze met his she felt undone. The air between them crackled with unsaid words, with years of longing and regret.

"Anne, I've been wanting to talk to you…" he started, but at that moment, JW burst out onto the patio with Louisa on his arm, both looking very drunk.

"Hey, Cap! Your girl here ain't looking too good," JW called out.

Louisa turned to Frederick, her expression uneasy. "I don't feel well, Cappy." Her words came out slowly and slurred. Frederick gently moved Louisa to a chair, and Anne's heart ached at their familiarity and his tenderness.

"I think I'm going to be sick," she moaned. Frederick looked around, a little panicked.

Anne stepped in. "Why don't I help her to the ladies' room?" she asked, and leaned down to help Louisa back up.

Louisa smiled. "Cappy said you were the sweeeetest…" she slurred as she leaned heavily onto Anne's arm.

Freddy let Anne take over. She gave him a small smile and supported Louisa back through the crowded bar and into the restrooms. As soon as they entered, Louisa turned to Anne and threw up all over her shoes.

"Oh, thank you, I feel so much better now," she said with a weak smile.

Anne looked down at the mess and sighed.

She, on the other hand, had never felt worse.

CHAPTER 25

Elizabeth

"I should infinitely prefer a book..."

- PRIDE AND PREJUDICE

Elizabeth left the Pump Room on her own and headed back toward the hotel lobby. She caught a glimpse of Anne and Frederick in conversation and couldn't help but wonder how that was going. Emma hadn't been ready to leave, which made Elizabeth chuckle. She knew her sister was probably put out at being upstaged by Jane's beautiful performance.

She entered the grand hall and walked over to its dual fireplaces to warm up from the cooler night air. As she stood there, she noticed a room across the hall that was lined with bookshelves. She made her way across the floor and entered the room cautiously.

It immediately took her breath away. Painted a dark green and lined from floor to ceiling with mahogany bookshelves, it reminded her of Belle's library from *Beauty and the Beast*. Like the grand hall, this room also had a fireplace that was giving off a warm glow. There was a large couch, several cozy chairs for guests to curl up in, and windows that provided a sweeping view of the gardens.

She couldn't believe she hadn't found this place sooner.

Giddy with excitement, she began looking at the titles on the shelves. Suddenly, she heard a gentle cough and was startled to see a man sitting in one of the chairs, a small lamp illuminating his spot. Darcy.

He had changed out of the suit he was wearing earlier and now appeared more relaxed and comfortable than she had ever seen him. He had a book on his lap, and he looked up at her with an amused smile.

"Oh, good grief, you startled me!" she said as she tried to get her racing heart back in line.

"I know, you seemed in your own world just now," he said, and that same amused smile replaced his normal scowl.

"I'm in awe of this room," she sighed, glancing around at the hundreds of books that surrounded her.

"It's my favorite spot in Mansfield," he said, looking around with the same admiration she felt. Elizabeth thought again about how for someone like Darcy, Mansfield was not a once-in-a-lifetime visit. He probably came here at least once a year, maybe more.

There was something about him that made her feel less sure of herself.

"I've always dreamed of having a library like this. Shelves full of beautiful books, a cozy spot next to a fire, a beautiful view," she said as she ran her hands over a leather-bound Charles Dickens first edition. She looked up to see Darcy studying her intently.

"So, what sparked this love of books?" he asked her as he placed the one he had been reading on the small table next to him, giving her his full attention.

"I think our parents instilled a love of reading into me and all my sisters. My mother would read to us at night. When we got older, she would still make us go to bed early, but we could stay up an extra hour if we were reading a book." Elizabeth smiled at the early memory of her mother. "Even after she passed, Elinor and I continued the tradition with our younger sisters. We all carried our love of books into our careers in some way. Elinor illustrates books, I edit them, and Anne became a librarian." She suddenly blushed. "I'm sorry, I didn't mean to bore you with my stories."

She quickly changed the subject. "Why did you leave so soon tonight?"

Darcy sighed and met her gaze. "I don't sing, and crowds aren't my thing. But you seemed to be having a good time." Elizabeth wasn't sure if she detected sarcasm or sadness in his tone. "Anyway, I tire of company much faster than I tire of a good book."

"I can leave if I'm disturbing you," she began.

"No!" he said, rather quickly, and she thought she noticed him blushing. "Don't feel you have to leave; I don't mind the company tonight."

She sat down near the fire, facing his chair. "So, what are you reading that you find better company than us?" she teased as she locked eyes with him.

He picked up the book and held it out so she could see the title.

"*Jane Eyre*! You're reading *Jane Eyre*?" she exclaimed, unable to hide her amazement.

"Didn't you accuse me on our date of only reading classics, and yet you're surprised to find me reading one?" he asked teasingly, his smile lighting up his whole face.

Elizabeth felt a little rush at his words. *Our date.* "I don't know. I expected Dickens or Trollope...or...or Collins," she stammered out.

"Who's the pretentious one now?" he asked as his eyebrow arched up. He was obviously enjoying this.

"I never called you pretentious!" she said indignantly

172

and blushed more deeply.

"Oh, you didn't have to. It was written all over your face that night," he replied. "Anyway, weren't you the one who suggested I read some romance?"

Elizabeth's voice rose in passion. "And you consider *Jane Eyre* a romance?" she asked incredulously. "Jane deserved better than Rochester." And she quoted from memory: "'I am a bird and no net ensnares me.'"

He continued to egg her on. "And yet, it has some of the most romantic and passionate dialogue for a novel of its time."

He picked up the book and read from the page, his voice low and raspy. "'Especially when you are near me as you are now. It feels as though I had a string tied here under my left rib where my heart is, tightly knotted to you in a similar fashion. And when you go to Ireland, with all that distance between us, I am afraid that this cord will be snapped, and I shall bleed inwardly.'" He stopped and held her gaze. Elizabeth felt her heart beating fast. "'Reader, I married him.' Isn't that the happily ever after you wanted? I thought for sure this would be one of your favorite romances."

Elizabeth stared at him, trying to figure out this enigma of a man, who could appear so gruff and unfriendly and moody. Yet, when relaxed, he could talk of a love of books and classics and romantic dialogue.

All she could think to say was, "I've never met a man who has read *Jane Eyre*."

"And you think I am the one who has all the prejudices," he chuckled as he shook his head.

Elizabeth lost all track of time as she and Darcy fell into easy conversation. When she finally glanced down at her watch, she was startled at how late it was. "I'd better head back; my sisters will be looking for me."

"Good night, Elizabeth," he said and returned to his

book.

She liked the way her name sounded coming from him. It gave her a rush of goosebumps. She headed up the grand staircase and walked back to her room.

Suddenly, she felt the urge to pick up a copy of *Jane Eyre*.

CHAPTER 26

Elinor

*"When so many hours have been spent convincing myself I
am right, is there not some reason to fear I may be wrong?"*

- SENSE AND SENSIBILITY

The next morning, Elinor looked out over the gray
clouds that were darkening by the minute. *Well, this
is not good*, she thought. Later this afternoon, they were
to have the wedding rehearsal and dinner down in the
gardens. She continued to glance up at the sky. The dark
clouds loomed heavy. There was no question they were
going to get some rain today.

She opened her laptop and checked to see if she had
any emails or messages from Eddie. Disappointment
swept over her again when she saw she had none. She
didn't know what she'd expected. Was she thinking he
would send her a text or message saying he was engaged?
No, she didn't think he would do that. He would want
to tell her in person. She couldn't help but wonder if he
would be excited or resigned when he told her the news.

She looked up as Elizabeth came out onto the balcony.

She, too, was frowning up at the clouds.

"I hope there is a plan B for today. It definitely looks like we are going to get some rain this afternoon. But I, for one, am glad. I think we should stay in and catch up. With all the activities, we haven't had the chance to really hang out together this trip. I think it's time you put away your computer, Emma puts away her phone, and we just talk and have some sister time."

Elinor sighed and closed her laptop. "Okay, but first we need coffee!"

"I've got us covered! Wake up the sleeping beauties, and I'll make a run downstairs to Mollands and get us coffee and sweets," Elizabeth said, referring to the famous bakery known for it's irresistible pastries and aromatic coffe. "I can smell those donuts from here!"

Thirty minutes later, the five of them were sitting out on the patio, loaded up with piping hot beignets and lattes, watching the sky darken and the thunder clouds roll in.

"OMG, these are seriously the best donuts I've ever had!" Catherine said, her lips now covered in powdered sugar.

"You're going to look like a snowman at the rate you're going, and they're French. They are not donuts, they are *beignets*," Elinor said. She laughed and took a cautious bite, careful not to get sugar all over herself while mocking her sister. She glanced over and watched as Emma staged her beignets and her latte on the patio table, and then proceeded to kneel down on the floor to capture the view in the background.

As Elinor watched, she said, "Em, seriously? Are you really letting hot beignets go to waste to take a picture?"

Emma was unfazed. "Mock me all you want, Elinor, but it pays my bills. This is too good of a photo op to pass up. Plus, if I tag the bakery, they will be happy to give us more." She typed out her caption and posted the photo.

Then she looked up to see her sisters staring at her. "I'm glad I have your attention anyway, because I really need your help tonight."

Elinor let out a groan. "I knew this was coming."

"Good, then you already know what I'm going to ask," Emma continued. "I really need some couples to promote the dating app. Mansfield is the absolute best location for great pics. I'm just asking you each to go online, pick a location here at the hotel, take a pic as a couple, and post it."

Elizabeth shot her sister a glaring look. "I assume this does not apply to me, since I already took one for the team with my date from hell."

"You are absolutely not off the hook, Lizzy. I can't believe you didn't even take one pic that night! The whole point was to get a pic of you and your date and post your meet-cute at the location," Emma said, not looking up as she scrolled through her phone.

"Silly me, I thought 'the point' of a dating app was to find someone with common interests," Elizabeth retorted with a smug look at Emma.

"That's what *you're* supposed to get out of it. I, on the other hand, am not looking for love. It's work…and I'm asking for your help." Emma looked pleadingly at all her sisters. "I was hoping tonight, with the rehearsal dinner, that each of you could do a little staged scene in a different location around the hotel with your dates."

Catherine let out a cloud of powdered sugar as she asked, "What 'dates' are you referring to?"

Emma responded matter-of-factly, "Well, the groomsmen, of course. We've each been paired up with a groomsman to walk us down the aisle, and we are seated with them for the rehearsal dinner tonight."

Anne eyed Emma suspiciously as she asked, "And how do you know this?"

"I may have had a little hand in assigning the matchups,"

Emma said, pleased with herself. They all groaned at once, but she exclaimed, "What! You're really going to complain about spending an evening with handsome, wealthy men?" Emma looked around at her sisters with a look of satisfaction on her face.

Elinor spoke up, her voice terse. "So, how are we paired up? Who are our 'dates'?"

"Lizzy, you will have the charming company of George Wickham. Anne, you have the handsomest date, Mr. William Elliot. And Elinor, you will have the delightful company of JW. And I'll be with Frank Churchill." Emma glanced nervously at Catherine. "I'm sorry, Kit Cat, but I had to pair one of us with Thorpe. I'm sure he will be on his best behavior!"

That was the final straw for Elinor. She couldn't hide her annoyance any longer. "Em, I really think this is going too far. I'm not the slightest bit interested in hanging out with any of the groomsmen beyond what is required for the wedding."

"You know, Elinor, somehow I just knew I wouldn't be able to count on you. Is it so hard to just try something new for one night?" Emma responded.

The words stung Elinor. She didn't feel like she was in the wrong, and she looked to her other sisters for support.

Instead of looking put out, she saw Catherine smiling as she said, "Oh, I just had the best idea! I saw they have carriage rides around the grounds. How about I sign up for one of those?"

Emma beamed. "That's a fantastic idea, Cat!"

Elinor felt her anger rising. "She already told you Thorpe's a jerk, and you're going to make her spend a 'romantic' evening with him just so you can get content for your dumb app?"

"Just because you don't get it, Elinor, doesn't mean you have to ruin it for everyone else," Emma said, frustration in her voice. "This is important to me, and whether you like it or not, it is my job."

Elinor couldn't hide the condescension in her voice. "I'm sorry, but posting on social media is not a real job."

Elizabeth interjected, "Really, Elinor, I think you're overreacting. This isn't a big deal, and it can help Emma. It could be fun."

Anne tried to ease the tension too. "I'll give it a go, Em. There are worse things than having to spend an evening with a good-looking, rich man."

Elinor felt frustrated. She was angry with Emma and couldn't understand why everyone else was so quick to support Emma's selfishness. "You know what? I need to log on to work for a bit. I'll catch up with you guys later." She quickly exited the patio and went into her room. For the second time on this vacation, she sobbed into her pillow.

A few minutes later Elinor heard Anne's concerned voice. "Here, let me get you a tissue." She reached over and extended a handful to Elinor.

"Why do I think this is about more than just what happened out there? What is going on with you on this trip? You haven't been yourself. You're moody and distant. We're worried about you." Anne's sympathetic face loomed over Elinor, who sat up in bed and faced her sister.

"I've managed to piss off all of you and ruin the morning. I think that's pretty on brand for me, wouldn't you say?" Elinor huffed back.

"You don't have to hold anything back with us, Elli. Maybe we can help. Sisters are supposed to tell each other what they are feeling."

"Is that why you haven't told me you changed your mind about going to graduate school?" Elinor asked belligerently. She had not intended to blurt that out, but she couldn't seem to stop herself from lashing out.

"Emma told me, since apparently you weren't going to."

Elinor saw Anne recoil a little as she said, "I didn't change my mind, Elli. I had never made it up in the first place. Graduate school was never my dream. I'm happy with where I am. And I was going to tell you, but we just haven't had much time together on this trip."

Elinor sighed and grabbed her sister's hand. "I only want you to be happy, Annie. I never meant to make you feel like you had to do something that didn't make you happy. And I'm not the only one keeping secrets this trip. Are you going to tell me what was going on with you the other night at the party?"

Anne sighed. "You know, you are good at turning things around on someone else. I came in here to see what was wrong with you, and you've got me spilling my guts." Anne did not look her sister in the eye but asked Elinor quietly, "Did you know Frederick was here?"

Elinor sat up straighter, pulling the pillows around her and gazing intently at her sister. "I did," she replied slowly. "But you broke up with him all those years ago. I didn't think…"

"I didn't break up with him, Elli. I refused his proposal because I didn't want to disappoint you. You were so adamant that I was making a mistake, and you convinced me to wait…but he wasn't willing to." Anne's voice faltered, and her tears started to fall. "I never stopped loving him, and now it's too late," she whispered.

Elinor pulled her sister in for a hug, feeling awash in guilt. "I never knew, Annie. I never knew you felt that way."

Anne pulled back and looked at her sister. "I know, that's why I'm here now. I know something is wrong, and you're holding it in." Anne studied her sister closely, all her usual reserve and stoicism gone. "Oh my god, you're in love!" Anne said, her eyes getting big and a grin taking over. A smile tugged at Elinor's face and then disappeared.

"I know," she groaned and then rolled back into the pillows.

"So, who is it?" Anne asked tenderly.

Before Elinor had a chance to respond, there was a small knock, and she looked up to see Elizabeth coming into the room, followed by Catherine and Emma.

"Are we done fighting? Today is a big day, and I think we just need to hug this out," Elizabeth said as she jumped onto the bed and playfully wrapped Anne and Elinor into a hug. Catherine and Emma jumped onto the bed too, and soon the sisters were all tangled up in arms and hugs. Their laughter instantly made Elinor feel better…and also relieved. She had been saved from answering Anne's question.

CHAPTER 27

Anne

"There, he had seen everything to exalt in his estimation the woman he had lost, and there begun to deplore the pride, the folly, the madness of resentment, which had kept him from trying to regain her when thrown in his way."

- PERSUASION

A loud, persistent knocking at the suite door startled them out of their laughter and Anne jumped up, answering it to reveal Mariah Bertram.

"Good grief, is this a scene out of *Little Women*? Please, pull yourselves together—we have a crisis going on," she said, sounding agitated and appearing more discomposed than they had ever seen her.

"What's happened, Mariah? What's wrong?" Anne asked with concern.

"Only the biggest disaster ever! That horrible Mr. Collins has taken ill. Food poisoning, apparently. So annoying! Anyway, he is out of commission," she wailed. "And look outside! The rehearsal dinner is in six hours, and it's supposed to be outside in the garden, but it is most definitely going to rain."

Anne marveled at how such a normally composed woman had been reduced to a whiny, petulant-sounding child.

"Can't we just move it to the tent?" asked Elinor, who attempted to compose herself as she grabbed at tissues.

"No. The tent is for the wedding-day dinner tomorrow. It's already set up and decorated. Mr. Collins set up the garden tables—he was convinced it wasn't going to rain. Now he's sick, and the rain is definitely coming. What a pompous ass! He was too arrogant to admit he screwed up. Who plans an outdoor rehearsal without a backup plan?" Mariah's normal composure and poise were completely gone.

"Cat, didn't you say your friend Henry works for the hotel?" Anne asked as she glanced over to Catherine. "Can you find him and figure out where we can move it inside?"

"I'm on it!" Catherine said, rushing out the door.

"Lizzy and Elinor, go see who you can find to help pull tables from the garden. Emma, find out which room when Cat returns, and be ready to redecorate when we bring everything in from the garden."

Mariah seemed to compose herself and looked gratefully at Anne. "Yes. Yes, I think this could work. I'll go tell Julia."

Anne was quite proud of what they had accomplished over the last hour and a half. Catherine had found Henry, who provided one of the terrace rooms as an alternative venue. Elizabeth and Elinor had rounded up several volunteers, who were loading up a truck with the tables and chairs, while most of the table decor had been delivered to Emma to redecorate.

She headed back down to the garden to retrieve the last handful of decorations. While walking, she felt the first drops of rain start to fall and held out her hand as she looked up. Now that their task was almost done, she didn't mind the rain.

Grabbing one last display, she started to make her way back when she caught sight of someone approaching, carrying a brightly colored umbrella. Her heart started pounding—it was Frederick. He stopped in front of her and extended the umbrella over both of them. It brought them close together, and she could feel the warmth of his body.

"Freddy, what are you doing here?" She looked timidly up into his eyes.

"I was told you saved the day," he said, smiling. "I thought you might still need help, but it looks like you are just about done. I thought I could at least offer you my umbrella." He was smiling down at her and handing the umbrella over to her. She grabbed the handle, and he took a step back. She immediately felt the loss of his presence. It felt colder.

He was now standing in the rain, but he didn't turn to leave. "Anne," he began, "about what you said last night." But as he spoke, Anne heard her name from another direction. She turned to see Will Elliot advancing toward them, his umbrella keeping him dry.

"There you are! Everyone is looking for you at the hotel. I hear you are to be my date for the evening." He shot a smug smile over to Frederick. "Come on, let's get you inside. I'll take it from here, Captain." He gave Frederick a nod and then reached over to take Anne's elbow, gently leading her away.

Anne looked back to see Frederick still standing in the same spot, the rain steady now. He didn't make an effort to move or walk away, but instead stood there, drenched in the pouring rain.

She thought of his words. *About what you said last*

night…

There could be no doubt he had overheard her conversation with Fanny.

CHAPTER 28

Elizabeth

*"Pleased with the preference of one, and offended by
the neglect of the other, on the very beginning of our
acquaintance, I have courted prepositions and ignorance,
and driven reason away, where either were concerned. Till
this moment I never knew myself."*

- PRIDE AND PREJUDICE

The sisters returned to their rooms with just enough time to get ready for the rehearsal. Elizabeth glanced out to the hotel balcony and down to the gardens below. The rain was really coming down hard now. She felt so proud of Anne for taking charge and putting a plan in motion. And from what she could tell before she came up, Emma had completely transformed the terrace room, making tonight's location seem like a scene out of a magical fairytale.

She was the first one ready, and since her sisters were still scrambling around to finish getting dressed, she decided to walk down to the rehearsal on her own. "I'm going to swing by the library and hang out there for a few minutes since I'm early," she said, although no one seemed to be paying attention. "Meet you all down there in thirty minutes."

She could kid herself and pretend she was going to the library to wait until it was time for the rehearsal, but she knew she was really hoping to find Darcy sitting in there again. She wasn't sure why, but she felt disappointed that he wouldn't be at the rehearsal. Tonight was to be a more intimate affair, just close family and members of the wedding party.

She thought of spending the evening with Wickham. They were to be partnered up for the walk down the aisle, as Emma had planned, and they would be seated together at dinner. She enjoyed his gregarious personality, so why was she thinking about Darcy?

She came upon the library, but tonight its double doors were shut. She opened one door slowly and looked in cautiously. The lights were out, and the only glow in the room was from the fireplace, which was emitting a soft orange glow across the room. As she started to enter, she heard someone moaning. At first, she thought someone might be hurt, but then she felt herself blush. That wasn't someone crying out in pain; that was someone moaning in pleasure.

Just across the room, up against the bookshelves, she could see the outline of a couple locked in a heated embrace. The woman had her back to Elizabeth, but the man was facing her. Neither of them had seen or heard her come in, but she could clearly see that the man was George Wickham. She suspected by the short brunette bob that the woman was Lydia. Elizabeth was mortified that she had walked in on them and disgusted that they had acted so carelessly.

Trying to tiptoe backward and make her way out of the room, she stumbled over the door. She saw Wickham look up and catch her eye. The woman turned around and looked completely unfazed at having been caught in the act. Elizabeth quickly turned around and shut the door. She heard Lydia burst out laughing and Wickham trying to shush her. She walked away, wishing she hadn't witnessed Wickham's extracurricular activities.

The sight left her unsettled, but relief washed over her as she spotted her sisters. Joining them, she stepped into the rehearsal hall. She marveled at how beautiful her sisters looked, but she was in absolute awe of what Emma had done with the room. The flowers had looked beautiful enough outside, but here in the smaller room, surrounded by glowing tea lights and vine-covered lanterns, it was nothing short of a fairytale ambiance.

Elinor, always keen to pick up on Elizabeth's moods, gave her a quizzical look. "You look a bit flustered," she said, eyeing Elizabeth carefully.

Elizabeth gave her an amused look. "Let's just say I found my partner for the evening a little indisposed." She leaned over and whispered to Elinor what she had seen in the library, and she couldn't help but laugh at Elinor's look of pure horror.

"I'm sorry, Lizzy. I thought you two had hit it off. I was kind of thinking you might enjoy tonight." Elinor seemed truly disappointed for her, and Elizabeth wasn't quite sure why she felt completely ambivalent.

Then there was some commotion as Fanny and Edmund arrived with the reverend. Elinor groaned—it was the pompous gentleman from the races.

"Where's the altar? How am I supposed to work without an altar?" Mr. Elton was glancing around the room, looking flustered and annoyed.

Elizabeth rolled her eyes, and Elinor laughed. "Well, this will be interesting."

They overheard Mariah explain that, because of the rain, the venue had been changed, and he would just have to make do. His countenance did not change, as if he held them all personally responsible for the weather.

"People, people, let's get started. If I could have the bride and groom up here near me, and the groomsmen to the right of the groom. Bridesmaids to the left of the bride."

Elizabeth and her sisters moved forward to line up beside Fanny. She overheard Mr. Elton lean over and ask Mariah, "Remind me again, what is the bride's name?"

Elizabeth groaned and wondered where the Bertrams had found this guy. What an arrogant jerk.

They all gathered and lined up as instructed. Elizabeth looked across at Wickham. He met her eyes and gave her a big grin and a wink. She rolled her eyes in disgust. He didn't appear the slightest bit fazed or embarrassed that, just twenty minutes ago, she had caught him pants down in the library.

She took in the rest of the groomsmen. She was pleased to see that George Knightley was Edmund's best man. She gave him a warm smile, and he gave her a gracious smile in return. It was hard for her to reconcile the teenage boy she had known with the man who was standing here, with graying temples and fierce blue eyes.

She looked over at Thorpe, who, not for the first time this week, looked like he'd had one too many drinks.

Will Elliot was looking straight at Anne, who appeared oblivious and was scanning the room as if looking for someone else.

Mr. Elton was trying to get their attention again. "People, why are we missing a groomsman? I simply can't work under these conditions," he groaned dramatically.

Elizabeth looked back over the groomsmen and realized it was JW who was missing. She leaned over and whispered to Elinor, "Where's JW?"

Elinor gave her a look of surprise and laughed back, "I haven't a clue, but maybe they should check the library."

Elizabeth snorted a laugh, which drew an immediate

look of disapproval from Mr. Elton.

Edmund and the groomsmen gathered into a huddle, and it was obvious no one knew where JW was. "Give me a few minutes," Edmund said. "I'm going to see if I can find a stand-in for now."

Elizabeth thought Mr. Elton was going to have an aneurysm. He let out an exaggerated sigh and threw his hands up in frustration.

Edmund leaned over and kissed Fanny. "I'll be right back," he told her, and then sprinted out the room.

Not for the first time, Elizabeth wondered how Fanny always appeared so unaffected by all the drama. She admired her cousin's composure. She wasn't sure that in the same circumstances she would be able to keep her mouth shut. As it was, she was about ready to tell Mr. Elton where he could stick his bible.

Edmund returned a few minutes later with a gentleman who was closer to Edmund's father's age than his own. "Everyone, this is an old friend of the family, Colonel Brandon."

For his part, Brandon seemed embarrassed and shy, but he stepped into place in the line. Elizabeth looked down at Elinor to gauge her reaction. Elinor leaned in and said, "I'm the only woman who could get ghosted by a man she's not even dating." Their subsequent giggles drew the immediate disapproving eye of Mr. Elton, again.

The rest of the rehearsal went off without a hitch, and soon the sisters found themselves seated for dinner at the long table, each next to a groomsmen. Elizabeth had decided she would not give Wickham the time of day and ignored him throughout the entire meal. She couldn't help thinking how wrong her first impression of him had been.

The same thought occurred to her about Darcy. Just four short days ago, she thought he was the biggest ass, and now she sat here wishing it were him she was sitting next to him instead of Wickham. How had she been so wrong?

CHAPTER 29

Emma

"Better be without sense than misapply it as you do."

- EMMA

They'd pulled off the rehearsal flawlessly, and Emma felt an immense sense of pride in what she had accomplished with the decorations in a short amount of time. Most of the table decorations had been ruined by the short rain shower, so she had improvised and sprinkled flower petals across the tables. She had asked Catherine for help, and Catherine had Henry find some unused garden lanterns.

The terrace room had been transformed, and it had the feel of an outdoor tea garden. She surprised herself with how much she'd enjoyed pulling it all together. They were now seated around the tables in the dim glow of tea lights. Bridesmaids and groomsmen were seated in pairs, as Emma had planned. She hoped her sisters were planning to take advantage of tonight to post to her app. She really needed some content, and this was just too good an opportunity to pass up. Emma had been uploading pictures to her stories all night, sharing the decorations and festivities. She was thrilled with the reactions from her followers and kept glancing down to see the comments.

So gorgeous

OMG you are so talented

Are you available for my wedding!?

She had to admit, reading all the positive reactions was giving her a high.

She glanced next to her at Frank Churchill. His eyes held her gaze, and Emma felt herself flush with heat.

"I was wondering when you were going to take your eyes off that phone. I was starting to feel neglected sitting here by myself."

"Not used to being ignored?" she teased and scooted her chair closer. She raised her phone. "How about a quick selfie of the two of us?" she asked, a wide smile on her face.

Frank pulled himself back out of the frame, startling Emma with his abruptness. "Sorry, it's just that I don't do social media. Not my thing," he said, rather awkwardly, as he sat up straight and grabbed his wineglass. "But hey, now that our duties here have been fulfilled, I was thinking maybe you and I could go somewhere a little quieter and get a proper drink." He gave Emma a big smile and wrapped his arm around the back of her chair, drawing them in closer again.

Emma had to admit, she was tempted. She had captured too many photos in this room and eyed the opportunity to photograph another spot on the hotel grounds at night.

Just as she was about to respond, she saw that Frank's attention had been drawn across the room. She looked across the crowded hall and saw that Jane Fairfax had just walked in. She wasn't one of the invited guests for the evening, but it was obvious she was looking for someone.

Jane's eye caught Emma's, and then she saw Frank.

Emma watched as a look of hurt fell across Jane's face. Then, she turned and abruptly left the room.

Frank immediately bounced up out of his chair. "Sorry, Emma, I'm going to have to take a rain check on that nightcap." He took one last long swig of his wine, set the glass down, and darted out of the room. Emma knew he was going after Jane. She wondered what the hell that could be about.

She felt frustrated. It wasn't that she was really interested in Frank's advances, but she hadn't intended for him to lose interest so easily. This also blew her plan to post on her app. She had counted on getting at least one picture with Frank that she could use for a fake post about a romantic night at the resort.

She looked out over the table to see how her sisters were doing. Elinor was talking to the colonel who had stood in for JW. That would never do—he was way too old for Elinor. One glance at Elizabeth and Wickham, and she knew her sister was not happy. She recognized that look. She wondered what could have happened there. She scowled and let out a big sigh.

"Well, come on now, it can't be that bad, can it?"

She looked up to see that Knightley had found his way to her. "I'm afraid it is." She tried to keep her voice from sounding childish. She didn't want to unload her thoughts on Knightley, but she found herself spilling her guts. "Nothing is going to plan. My sisters are supposed to be helping me create some romantic posts with their dates, but they all look bored, disinterested, or, even worse, disgusted."

He slid into the seat next to her. "Did you really think playing matchmaker with the groomsmen was going to work?" he asked, more amused than critical.

"Well, why wouldn't it? The setting is romantic, the wine is flowing, they have to spend the evening in each other's company," she answered, a tone of defensiveness in her voice.

"Did you include yourself in this little project?" he asked as his lip lifted into a smile.

"As a matter of fact, I did!" she replied petulantly. "Frank has been hitting on me all week, but as soon as I asked him to pose with me, he started acting strange."

Knightley looked at her with a huge smile. "Well, maybe he was afraid his fiancée would see him with you on social media."

Emma couldn't hide her surprise. Her mouth dropped open, and her eyes went wide. "Wait, Frank is engaged? To *whom*?"

"To Jane, of course, and she deserves a lot better than him, if you ask me."

"But he…" she started to say.

"I know, it's nothing new. He swears he will straighten up when it's official, but, like I said, Jane deserves better. His grandmother holds the purse strings, and she would never approve of a girl like Jane. So, he just continues to string her along until he wins his grandmother over, or until she dies and leaves him all her money."

Emma felt a repulsion for Frank and a newfound sympathy for Jane.

"Let's keep going down your list. You put poor little Catherine with that drunk Thorpe?" He gave Emma a disapproving look. "Badly done, Emma."

"I know, that one was unfortunate. But Cat makes the best of every situation, and I figured she would mind the least of all my sisters. In my defense, I wasn't counting on her to help much tonight."

Just then, she saw Anne and Will Elliot moving to the dance floor. She looked smugly at Knightley. "Ah-ha! All is not lost yet," she said, pointing to the couple, who were now slow dancing.

Knightley watched them with interest. "Hate to say it, but I wouldn't put my money on Will. He's always looking out for himself and what he can gain from a situation. He's got an ax to grind with his uncle. Nothing's more important to him than showing he can fit into his uncle's world. I'm guessing he thinks your sister comes from money. Her friendship with the Crofts is also to his advantage. Plus, it's obvious Anne is pining over the captain. She hasn't taken her eyes off him all week."

Emma looked at him, completely clueless. "The captain? You mean Freddy?" she asked, stunned at this revelation.

He looked back at her just as curiously. "You really have no clue what's going on around you, do you? If you took your nose out of your phone and paid attention, you would see it. And if I'm reading the situation right, I'd say Frederick Wentworth has it bad for her as well."

"Freddy is interested in Anne?" she mused, and then she recalled the first night here, how Anne had been upset. Had there been something going on between her and Freddy?

"I'm sorry. I think I spoiled your evening, but a matchmaker you are not, Emma!" he scolded her gently. He took a look around the room and then looked her in the eyes. She noticed for the first time how beautifully blue his eyes were, and she had the sudden realization that she found him attractive. Infuriating, but attractive.

"You are, however, a very talented wedding decorator," he said, admiring the room. He leaned toward her and whispered, "Get off that phone, and who knows what you could do."

Definitely more infuriating than attractive! she thought.

CHAPTER 30

Catherine

"And from the whole she deduced this useful lesson, that to go previously engaged to a ball, does not necessarily increase either the dignity or enjoyment of a young lady."

- NORTHANGER ABBEY

Catherine couldn't get over how beautiful the room looked. What an amazing job her sisters had done to pull off what could have been a disaster! The rehearsal went beautifully. They used the indoor stage in lieu of tomorrow's wisteria arch. Each bridesmaid and groomsman rehearsed their walk down the aisle. Fanny and Edmund seemed so in love and so excited for their big day tomorrow. The dinner was delicious, dessert incredible, and she even had a glass of wine. It would have been a picture-perfect evening...except for the fact that she was seated next to John Thorpe.

He had been an insufferable bore throughout the whole meal. She was sure she had not said four words the entire time. And, as usual, she had found him to be rude and obnoxious.

For his part, Thorpe didn't seem to notice Catherine's indifference. He continued to talk and drink his way through the meal, and she simply couldn't wait for it to be over.

She was thrilled with the idea she had come up with to help Emma with her dating site. The resort offered horse-drawn carriage rides around the gardens in the evening, and Catherine had reserved a ride, only not with Thorpe. Luckily, the weather had cleared up in the last hour, and she texted Henry to ask if he would like to accompany her. She was excited when he said he would love to. Now, she was just waiting for him to get off work, and then she would meet him down in the gardens. In the meantime, Thorpe was making a pest of himself.

She had made plans to meet Henry at 7:15 p.m. It was ten after seven, and as she hurriedly made her way down the path, she heard Thorpe come running after her.

"Leaving so soon? I thought we could spend more time getting to know each other," he said as he caught up to her.

The carriage was waiting, and she felt relieved that she hadn't missed it. "Look, I'm sorry, John, but I've already made plans for the evening." She tried to brush past him into the carriage but he blocked her way. "I've already reserved this ride."

He appeared completely unfazed. "Great! I'll join you."

Flustered, she looked around and said, "Well, I'm supposed to meet someone here." But Henry wasn't there yet. And, before she could resist any further, Thorpe had hoisted himself up into the carriage and was extending his hand to help her up.

"Looks like your date is a no-show. Guess you will have to settle for me." He gave her a wink and settled into the carriage seat.

Catherine started to take the seat across from him, but

he pulled her toward him. The carriage started to move, and Catherine looked around desperately to see if Henry had arrived, but he was still nowhere to be seen.

She was feeling frustrated about missing Henry and irritated with John's aggressive behavior. She pushed herself farther away from him.

"Oh, c'mon, you're not going to sulk, are you?" he asked. He reached into his pocket and pulled out a flask, took a big swig, then offered it to her.

"No thank you, and from the looks of it, you don't need any more either," she said, no longer trying to hide her irritation.

"Don't be such a bore," he said nastily. He took another big swig. "I can't believe I got the sister who's such a prude," he whined.

She pretended to ignore him but grew more uncomfortable the more he drank. She pulled out her phone and saw that she had missed a text and a call from Henry.

Sorry I got off late and missed the ride. Heading home but see you tomorrow?

Catherine felt the tears well up in frustration. Tomorrow was their last full day, and it was the wedding. She doubted she would get to see Henry much, if at all. She had been looking forward to spending this evening with him, and the carriage ride was the perfect opportunity to help Emma.

This was all Thorpe's fault, and she found her anger rising. As the carriage took a turn, she felt Thorpe move over, and before she could respond, he leaned in and started kissing her.

For once, Catherine lost her timidity. The shock of the kiss, the frustration of the evening, and Thorpe's obnoxious behavior came to a head, and before she knew it, she threw a punch, one that landed right on his nose.

He pulled back in pain, and his hand flew to his

bleeding nose. "You broke my nose! Do you have any idea what you just did? I can't believe you broke my nose!" The blood started coming through his fingers, and the full impact of what she had done hit her.

"You deserved it. Maybe next time you'll keep your hands to yourself!"

In all the commotion, the driver had stopped the carriage, and Catherine shakily stepped down the steps and got off. She felt a little dazed and stumbled to catch her footing when a hand reached over and steadied her. She looked up to see a tall gentleman in a blue tracksuit.

He was breathless and had obviously been on a run. He glanced into the carriage and caught sight of Thorpe, who was still holding his bleeding nose.

"Are you alright?" the man asked urgently.

Catherine nodded as she continued to try and steady herself on her feet.

"Lean on me," he said, and he leaned over to offer his arm. "I'll walk you back."

She glanced back to see Thorpe still in the carriage, bleeding and cursing.

CHAPTER 31

Anne

"She had been forced into prudence in her youth, she learned romance as she grew older: the natural sequel of an unnatural beginning."

- PERSUASION

Anne couldn't help herself. She looked around the beautifully lit room yet again, hoping to see Frederick. She knew it was a smaller party tonight, but the Crofts were here, and she hoped that meant Frederick might have been invited.

She could not get the scene from the garden earlier in the day out of her head. She felt a rising frustration with Will. Why was he always popping up whenever she had an opportunity to talk to Freddy? She should have been flattered by the attention, but while she found Will charming and good-looking, she just couldn't bring herself to be interested in him. Then her frustration switched to Emma, for putting them all on the spot tonight and trying to matchmake by setting them up with the groomsmen.

Will returned with a glass of wine and handed it to her. "Cheers to Fanny and Edmund," he said, leaning over to clink his glass with hers.

"Cheers to their happiness," she said, and she suddenly felt guilty for being irritated with him.

"So, Anne, tell me how long you've known the Crofts." His gaze steadily held hers as he took a sip of his wine.

"The Crofts?" Anne asked, confused. "I just met them the other day. I met Sophie down at the pool, and she introduced me to the admiral that day at the races."

"Oh," he said, and now he appeared to be confused. "I was under the impression you worked with them on the campaign."

"Not at all," Anne said, letting out a little laugh. "I'm a librarian, and I work in my hometown's library."

"You mean you volunteer at the library?" he asked.

Now she was the one confused. "Volunteer? If I volunteered, how would I pay my bills?" She laughed again.

"I guess I assumed that, as a relative of the Bertrams, you were independently wealthy. I wouldn't think you could stay here on a librarian's salary, either."

Anne looked at him, amused. "Oh, you've made all kinds of wrong assumptions," she said. "My sisters and I are related to Fanny. We have no relationship with the Bertrams except through her. They were kind enough to pay for our stay here at Mansfield. I don't think I would ever have dreamed of staying somewhere this nice." She thought she perceived just the smallest change in Will's smile. It seemed tight, almost forced. "Sorry to disappoint you," she said, smiling up at him.

"Oh, don't be silly," he said. "I was obviously under misguided assumptions."

The awkward conversation was cut short as Elinor approached them. "What a beautiful night it turned out to be after all," she said to both of them, in an attempt to start a conversation.

Will looked at Anne and then at Elinor. "I'll leave you two ladies to catch up. If you'll excuse me."

Elinor looked at Anne quizzically. "I'm sorry, did I scare him off?"

Anne let out a little sigh. "No, I think Will's interest in me was solely based on him thinking I was someone I'm not. I think he's gone off to nurse his disappointment, and something tells me he won't be back."

Elinor looked at Anne. "I'm sorry, sis. You looked like you two were getting along so well. I thought maybe he was taking your mind off other things."

Anne just smiled. She realized that even after all this time, Elinor still did not understand her love for Freddy. She changed the subject and asked, "So, what do you think happened to JW tonight? I'm sorry you got stuck with Colonel Brandon."

Elinor smiled. "I can't really complain. I have to admit, I rather enjoyed the colonel's company. Plus, I got the tea on JW's sudden departure."

"Oh, spill it, spill it!" she said with a little too much glee.

"It sounds like the big Texan was in arrears with outstanding child support, for a son no one knew he had. When he got wind he was about to be served, he disappeared."

Anne was appalled. "Ugh, what a creep. That's so disappointing, because I really liked him. Just goes to show, you never really know what people have going on. Plus, I think Emma is going to kill us for not getting any pics for her app," Anne said, half serious and half worried about Emma's reaction.

"Well, that's what she gets for coming up with such a stupid idea in the first place. I don't feel bad for her at all. I'm fed up with her matchmaking," Elinor said, a little too indignantly.

Anne looked boldly at her oldest sister. For once, she felt ready to speak her mind.

"You know, Elli, Emma's right. You don't have to keep watching over us anymore. We're all grown up; we can make our own choices and decisions. Emma's passionate about what she's doing. Why can't you just accept this is what she wants to do with her life right now?"

Elinor's eyes filled with hurt. "I can't seem to say the right thing to any of you."

Anne reached over to hug her. "Quit trying so hard all the time, sis. It's okay to just let things go once in a while and trust that we are going to be fine."

Elinor shook her head and nodded in agreement, but Anne could tell she was upset by her frankness.

"I think I'm going to go find something to drink," Elinor said, in an obvious attempt to avoid any further discussion.

Anne watched her sister go, and while she felt a little pang of guilt, she also felt a sense of relief. It felt good to get what she was thinking off her chest.

Without Will or Elinor around, she resumed looking around the room again in hopes that Frederick had arrived.

"Looking for anyone in particular?" she heard, and she turned to see Mrs. Croft with a hint of amusement in her smile.

Anne blushed. "Hi, Sophie, and no, I was just looking around."

"Uh-huh." Mrs. Croft smiled, giving her a knowing glance. "He's not here tonight, but he will be at the wedding tomorrow."

"Oh, who is that?" Anne replied, trying to act nonchalant.

"Honey, it's written all over your face every time he's around. And I'm not talking about Will. You, my dear girl, are in love with Frederick."

Anne looked at the kind, motherly woman and felt a surge of appreciation. "I know," she practically whispered. "But it's too late. I lost him years ago, and I don't think I can get him back."

"Oh, I wouldn't be so sure of that, honey. Men don't forget as much as we think they do. They just take longer to forgive. I've been watching Frederick this week, and if I had to guess, I would say he's just as in love with you as you are with him. You both just need to talk things through."

Anne felt her heart soar at Sophie's words. She resolved to talk to Freddy tomorrow, at the wedding. Maybe he couldn't forgive her, but she had to know for sure, and she had to tell him how she felt. She just needed to find the right opportunity.

CHAPTER 32

Elinor

"But to appear happy when I am so miserable – Oh! who can require it?"

- SENSE AND SENSIBILITY

Elinor was ready for the evening to be over. The conversation with Anne was just one more in what had been a very long day.

She just had to make it through one more day, she told herself. She needed to get home, see Eddie, and hear directly from him that he was truly going to go ahead with marrying Lucy. She was having an internal struggle. Would she try to talk him out of it? Would she confess her feelings for him? Did he have feelings for her? It was all too much to think about. The strain was starting to get to her.

She was startled out of her thoughts by a little commotion at the front of the room. She looked up to see Catherine walking in, leaning on the arm of a gentleman she did not recognize. It was not someone from the party, as he looked to have been out on a run. He was tall and scowling but seemed to be guiding Catherine to a chair. He caught Elizabeth's eye and waved her over. Elinor got up and made her way toward the three of them, but Elizabeth got there first. She seemed to know the man, and she directed her questions to him.

"Darcy, what's happened? Is Catherine okay?" She fired off questions, concerned.

Darcy looked at them and started to explain. "She's fine, just a little shaken up. The kid is stronger than she looks," he said, and gave Catherine a wink.

She looked up with a weak smile. "I'm fine," she said. "I was on the carriage ride, and Thorpe insisted on joining me, and, well, he's had too much to drink," she said shakily easing back into the chair.

Elizabeth jumped in, fire in her eyes. "Did he hurt you?"

"No, no, he just tried to make a pass, but I was able to push him off."

Darcy laughed, "She did more than push him off. I think she broke his nose."

"You hit him?" Elinor asked incredulously.

Catherine nodded and said, "I've been taking self-defense classes. You don't listen to true crime podcasts and not know how to defend yourself." She smiled bravely as she added, "I just never thought I would have to put it to use here."

By this time, both Anne and Emma had walked over to see what all the commotion was about.

"What were you doing out by yourself anyway?" Elinor asked, with more irritation in her voice than concern.

"I was supposed to meet Henry. We were going to go on a carriage ride, but he was held up with work, and Thorpe followed me out. Really, it's no big deal." Catherine looked gratefully up at Darcy as she said, "Thank you so much for walking me back. It was very kind of you."

"I'm just glad you're okay. Looks like you're in good hands now," Darcy said, his voice low and tender.

As he turned to leave, Elinor caught the prolonged gaze between him and Elizabeth.

Elinor was fuming, but she wasn't sure who she felt more mad at: Catherine for acting so carelessly, or Emma for encouraging it.

Elinor turned to Emma. "This is all your fault. What the hell were you thinking pairing her with someone like Thorpe? If you hadn't kept pressuring us to use your dating app, she never would have put herself in this situation." Okay, so apparently it was Emma she was mad at.

Emma started to defend herself, but instead welled up with emotion and turned to walk away.

Elinor wanted to stop, but she couldn't seem to rein in all her frustration. "And you," she said, turning to Catherine. "Who is Henry? And why were you going out with him without telling us?"

If Elinor had expected Emma to fight back, she definitely had not expected Catherine to.

"First of all, Elinor, I'm not a child anymore. Second, if you had bothered to ask me sooner, you would know who Henry is." She stood up, and Anne wrapped one arm around her shoulder and guided her out of the room.

Elinor felt the heat from Elizabeth's stare.

"Don't start on me," Elizabeth said with a weak smile. "I haven't done anything."

CHAPTER 33

Emma

"She looked back as well as she could; but it was all confusion.

She had taken up the idea, she supposed and made everything bend to it."

— EMMA

Fanny's wedding day was here! Emma looked out the window and saw that it was going to be a gorgeous day. All the rain and gloom from yesterday had been swept away, and the sun was out.

She tried to feel motivated to get up, but she had not slept well. Elinor's anger with her last night and her conversation with George Knightley were weighing heavily on her conscience. She had misread so much, and now it felt like all her sisters' unhappiness was on account of those misunderstandings. This was their last day together, and she didn't want it spoiled.

She looked over at Anne and Catherine, still asleep, and quietly got up. But a knock at the door startled them awake.

Anne groaned, "If that's Mariah again with some emergency, DO NOT OPEN THAT DOOR!" and she pulled a pillow over her head.

Emma cracked the door, peeked through, and let out a squeal of joy.

"It's Fanny!" she exclaimed, and she pulled the door wide open to reveal their cousin. Fanny entered, looking radiant and smiling from ear to ear.

"Happy wedding day!" Catherine yelled out from the bed as she scrambled to get up.

Elinor and Elizabeth came through the adjoining suite door, and they all rushed to give her a hug.

"We've barely had any time with you this whole trip!" Elizabeth exclaimed.

Fanny sighed. "I know, I'm so sorry. This week has been a blur, and I know tonight will be crazy, so I was hoping you were all available today. I have a surprise for you." Her bright eyes sparkled mischievously.

"Why are you doing anything for us? This is *your* day; we are celebrating you!" Elinor exclaimed.

Fanny looked lovingly at her cousins. "I'm just so appreciative that you are here, especially with everything you've had to put up with this week. Flaky wedding planners, missing groomsmen, that horrible clergyman, all of Edmund's crazy relatives." She let out a little giggle. "Anyway, I thought we could all spend the morning together. Mrs. Bertram arranged for us to have our hair and makeup done together. So come on, get dressed. Let's go!"

An hour later, Emma and her sisters found themselves in the bridal suite, which had been set up to provide makeup and manicures.

"Alright, ladies, let's enjoy some pampering while we catch up," Fanny said, sitting down to have a pedicure. "I want to hear all about your love lives! Catherine, I hear you had quite an adventure last night."

Emma cringed. She hoped this wouldn't set Elinor off on another rant. She looked over and was relieved to see that her sister appeared relaxed and happy. This was just what they all needed, and she could have hugged Fanny for giving them this time together before the wedding.

Emma looked over to Catherine, who seemed fine after last night's fiasco. Catherine looked shyly over to Fanny.

"As a matter of fact, I have met someone! I met him here at Mansfield. He's one of the assistant managers of the resort."

Fanny beamed. "Oh, you must mean Henry!" she said.

"You know him?" Catherine asked, surprised.

"Yes, he's been so wonderful during our stay here. So accommodating and helpful, and he's very, very cute," she said, giving Catherine a knowing look.

Catherine blushed. "He is, isn't he? I was supposed to meet him last night for another date, but he had to work late. That's how I ended up with Thorpe."

Emma glanced over as she asked, "A second date? What was your first date? How do I not know about this guy?"

"With everything going on this week, we haven't really had time to talk. I wanted to tell you all about it but…well, it's been crazy. Did y'all know that one of the rooms here at Mansfield is haunted?" she asked, and she proceeded to tell her sisters and cousin of her adventure in Room 813.

At the end of her story, Emma gasped. "That is the best meet-cute I've heard!"

Elizabeth laughed. "I think what she's saying, Cat, is that would make a great post on her dating app."

"Nope, no more pressure, I promise," Emma replied

with a sigh.

"What about you, Lizzy? What's going on with you?" Fanny inquired, her tone inquisitive. Emma felt a flicker of jealousy, realizing that Fanny was effortlessly coaxing out of her sisters what they had not managed to divulge on their own.

"Well, mine is not quite a meet-cute story like Catherine's. In fact, I think my story might be an enemies to..." She hesitated, then said, "An enemies-to-friends story. Do y'all remember the horrible date I told you about, with the conceited jerk?"

Emma glowered at her. "How could I forget the ranting voice messages you left me!?"

Elizabeth laughed. "Well, would you believe me if I told you he was here at Mansfield?"

Fanny giggled. "Well, conceited jerks are not in short supply here, so, yes, I'd believe you. But that description doesn't really narrow it down." Then a smile spread across Fanny's face, as if she'd just realized something.

"It wasn't Wickham, was it?" Anne asked. All the sisters were intensely curious now.

With a look of disgust, Elizabeth replied, "Ugh, no, but how I didn't see that guy was a jerk sooner, I'll never know."

Elinor spoke up. "It was the guy who walked Catherine back last night, wasn't it?"

Elizabeth looked over to her. "Yes, that was Darcy, but how did you know?"

Elinor smiled at her sister. "The way he looked at you, it was obvious he was into you."

Catherine quickly jumped in. "Why did you say he was a jerk, Lizzy? He was so kind and sweet with me last night. I don't know why you would think he was arrogant."

Elizabeth sighed. "I know. I think my first impression was completely wrong, and I'm the one who's been a jerk to him. Now, I'm starting to think I might like him, but I'm pretty sure he can't stand me. Anyway, I've made a mess of the whole thing, so there really is nothing to tell."

Fanny gave her a knowing smile as she said, "Oh, I heard his side of the story of that date, and I wouldn't be too sure of that!"

Then she turned her knowing gaze onto Anne. "And, Annie, I know all about your love interest. Sophie Croft has been keeping me apprised of you and Freddy."

Anne let out a soft sigh. "We really haven't had a chance to talk. It feels like every time we come close, something interrupts us. I'm sort of hoping I'll be able to talk to him at the wedding today."

Emma felt yet another pang of regret. Knightley had been right when he told her last night that Anne was still interested in Frederick. Why had she not seen it? Worse yet, why had she been pushing Anne toward Will?

"Don't think you're off the hook, Elinor. What story do you have for us?" Fanny asked.

At first, Emma thought Elinor was going to brush it off. She couldn't recall ever hearing Elinor tell them about a man she was interested in. Elinor only ever talked about work.

She saw Elinor struggle for composure, and then she burst into tears. Everyone was so shocked, they didn't say anything for a minute. Then Elizabeth got up and put her arms around her.

Elinor finally said, "I'm so sorry. I didn't mean for that to happen, and I certainly don't want to put a damper on your day, Fanny." Elinor tried to quickly regain her composure.

Fanny nodded, looking wise beyond her years. She quietly prodded, "Tell us all about him."

Elinor took a deep breath and told them everything. About Eddie, his obligation to his family, her deepening feelings for him, how she saw Lucy's post their first night at Mansfield, and how she had not heard from him since. Fanny and the sisters listened in shocked silence.

Finally, Elizabeth spoke up. "Why would you not tell us, Elli? It's not good to keep all these feelings bottled up."

Elinor looked at her sisters. "Because I'm the one who should be there for you guys. I shouldn't be putting my burdens on you."

Anne got up and hugged Elinor. "We are here for you, Elli. Don't shut us out anymore."

Emma looked over to Elinor. "Are you still mad at me?" she asked meekly.

Elinor smiled brightly. "No, I'm not mad at you. But I think you're the only one who hasn't shared a story."

Emma thought about it for a minute. "I'm afraid I'm going to disappoint you all. I don't think I've ever been in love, and I'm starting to think I never will."

Fanny looked at her skeptically. "So, there's absolutely no one who even sparks an interest?"

Emma emphatically shook her head no, but in the back of her mind she thought of a pair of intense blue eyes that had held her gaze for a little too long last night.

She looked up to see Fanny watching her, and she had the uncanny feeling that Fanny knew exactly who she was thinking of. Eager to change the subject, Emma exclaimed, "Wait, I don't think you ever told us yours and Edmund's story. That last summer we spent with you, you both were just friends. Fill us in on what we missed!"

Fanny smiled. "Well, first of all, I have all of you to thank for ever even meeting Edmund. Especially you, Emma," she said, eyeing Emma warmly.

Emma looked up, surprised. "Me? Why, what did I do?"

"I had already spent two summers there on my stepmother's estate, and I had never mustered the courage to talk to anyone or meet the neighbors. But the first summer you all came to visit, you insisted we get out and do things. As soon as you saw there were other kids around, you made us all introduce ourselves. From that point on, the Bertrams were my friends. Well, at least Edmund was." She laughed. "I think Mariah and Julia just tolerated me because Edmund made them be nice to me. He was so kind to me in those early years, and I'm pretty sure he looked at me as a younger sister back then. And I adored him. He was the kindest, most patient person I had ever met. My father worked all the time, and my stepmother made it clear I was not wanted. Edmund paid attention to me, made me feel special, and if it wasn't for him I'm not sure how I would have made it through those unhappy years." She paused, and Emma realized she had never understood what her cousin had gone through.

"Anyway," Fanny continued, "when my father passed, my stepmother kicked me out. I was a bit lost. I thought maybe I would come stay with you all, but then the Bertrams offered to take me in. Edmund said he was looking for someone to take care of his mom since he and his sisters were away at school so much. Truthfully, I was happy to do it."

Elizabeth exclaimed in shock, "You went to live with the Bertrams?" Her expression hardly concealed her horror at the thought. "Oh my god, this all sounds straight out of a Dickens novel," she teased.

Fanny laughed. "It's not as terrible as you make it out to be, Lizzy. The Bertrams became like family to me. I mean, Mariah and Julia can be a bit much at times, but I think they were just grateful to have someone look after their mother. And Mrs. Bertram really is so sweet. She can be quite good company when she's not too loopy."

Catherine chimed in, "But what about Mr. Bertram? He used to terrify me when we were kids. Frankly, he's still pretty scary, even now."

Fanny laughed again. "Oh, his bark is way worse than his bite. He's actually a big teddy bear once you get to know him."

"I can't believe you never told us, Fanny. We would have taken you in in a heartbeat." Elinor was visibly upset that they had never known of Fanny's situation. They had always assumed she'd remained with her stepmother.

Fanny smiled shyly. "But see, by that point, I already knew I was in love with Edmund. I had no hope it was mutual, but I just wanted to be near him. When he was home over the holidays or on weekends, we would spend time together. I think he was confused about what he wanted to do with his life. And I was someone he could confide in, talk to. I think, over time, he came to feel about me as I had always felt about him." Fanny continued, "So you see? It's not really a Dickens tale at all—it has a happy ending."

Emma felt a rush of shame come over her. She had spent all these years envying Fanny for living a life Emma thought she wanted, when all along she had something Fanny didn't: the company and love of her sisters. It saddened her to think of how lonely Fanny must have been all those years. Feeling overcome with emotions, she reached over and gave a startled Fanny a huge hug.

The rest of the day flew by in a blur of manicures, makeup, updos, and lots of laughter.

"I have one last surprise for you," Fanny said, opening a closet door to reveal the bridesmaids' dresses. "I hope you love them as much as I do," she said, beaming.

Emma gave a gasp of joy at the sight of her bridesmaid dress. She ran her fingers over the silky golden peach fabric, inspecting the intricate beadwork and delicate lace of her gown. It was more gorgeous than even she could have imagined. She looked at the beautiful dresses for her sisters, each unique in design but matching in varying shades of peach and orange. Then her eyes landed on the wedding dress, and she reached out to touch the lustrous satin.

"Oh my God, Fanny! Is this Vivienne Westwood?" Emma exclaimed.

CHAPTER 34

Fanny

"Her heart was made for love and kindness, not for resentment."

- MANSFIELD PARK

Fanny looked at each of her cousins standing before her, their bridesmaid dresses complimenting them perfectly. A wave of gratitude washed over her, she couldn't imagine this day without them.

Now, it was her turn. She slipped into the adjoining room to put on her wedding dress.

Spending the day getting ready with her cousins had been just what she needed. Lots of stories, laughter, and love. They grounded her after a week of craziness.

The week at Mansfield had given them a glimpse of the life Fanny was taking on, and she could see the worry etched on their faces. She knew her cousins better than they thought she did. She knew Elinor well enough to know that she thought Fanny was entirely too young to be getting married. And Elizabeth had never been good at concealing her disapproval for those who flaunted their wealth. But she knew their concern was out of love, not judgment. They were worried for her, and Fanny could understand how it looked from the outside.

There was very little about this day that had been of her own choosing. If she and Edmund had their way, they would have been married months ago, in a small church wedding with little fanfare. But they both understood his family's expectations, and so they put up little resistance to the proposed plans. The truth was, for the most part, she was indifferent to the plans. Most people would not understand her lack of interest in the arrangements for her own wedding day. But she had never been one to care about extravagance or status. For Fanny, big wedding or small wedding, it didn't matter, as long as it was Edmund at the altar waiting for her.

So she let Mariah and Julia pick the venue, the decorations, the flowers, almost everything. She had only put her foot down on two requirements. She wanted her cousins to be her bridesmaids, and she would pick out her own wedding dress—especially after Mariah's insistence on a baroque mini dress and Julia's horrifying preference for everything taffeta.

In the end, she chose an ivory trumpet silhouette made of silk and delicately decorated with pearls down the low back. A small train and a long, lace-edge Juliet veil completed the look. It was simple and elegant.

Now, as she took in her reflection in the mirror, she felt a sense of satisfaction. Stepping out of the suite's bridal room, it was her turn to present herself to her cousins. "Well, what do you think?" she asked, scanning their faces for approval.

Catherine gasped and raised her hands to her mouth.

Anne smiled at her, tears welling in her eyes. "Wow, Fanny. You look gorgeous."

"I want to hug you, but I'm afraid to!" Elinor exclaimed.

Emma gazed upon her adoringly. "Fanny, I've never

seen a more beautiful bride." She said it with such genuine approval that Fanny knew she had gotten it right.

They all came together to give her a big hug. Her heart swelled with happiness and gratitude.

"You can't make me cry! You'll ruin my makeup," she said, but the tears were already coming.

Following her bridesmaids to the gardens, Fanny tried to take in every detail of the moment. Small outdoor lanterns covered in ivy, baby's breath, and small white and pink roses lit the way down the aisle. The altar was not one but three overlapping flower arches, each decorated with all different shades of pink and red roses. The view through the arches looked out onto Mansfield's lake. To the right was the large tent strung with fairy lights that would host the reception late into the evening. The tables were beautifully decorated with elegant vases that were filled with the same pink and white roses that hung on the lanterns.

As she prepared to walk down the aisle, she clutched tightly to her bouquet and felt a rising nervousness at being the center of attention. But then, she caught sight of Edmund. His eyes met hers, and they were so full of warmth and love that she immediately felt herself grow calmer and more confident. He smiled at her, and she beamed back at him. No matter how many ways she had dreamed of her wedding day, she never once imagined it would be this beautiful. But in her dreams, it was always Edmund waiting for her at the altar. It had always been Edmund.

CHAPTER 35

Catherine

"The anxiety, which in this state of their attachment must be the portion of Henry and Catherine, and of all who loved either, as to its final event, can hardly extend, I fear, to the bosom of my readers, who will see in the tell-tale compression of the pages before them, that we are all hastening together to perfect felicity."

- NORTHANGER ABBEY

C atherine dabbed her eyes as she watched her beautiful cousin walk down the aisle and exchange vows with Edmund. The day was absolute perfection...well, almost. She did have to be accompanied down the aisle by Thorpe, who was sporting a bandage across the bridge of his nose and who appeared very polite and contrite with Catherine. She guessed that, for once, he might be sober. She felt a little pang of regret that his damaged face would be forever memorialized in Fanny's wedding photos. But only a little pang.

She looked out over the audience. It truly was all of Edmund's relatives and friends. She realized why it had been so important to Fanny for the sisters to be here for her. She knew the day they had all spent together was a memory she would always treasure. Catherine felt a feeling of happiness spread over her.

Her only regret for the day was that she wouldn't have the opportunity to see Henry and explain last night's fiasco with Thorpe. It mortified her to think that he might believe she would rather have spent the evening with Thorpe than with him.

With the ceremony coming to an end, Catherine realized she had not eaten all day. She walked toward the hors d'oeuvres, picked up a plate, and heard a voice behind her.

"I hear the sweet potato pies are delicious."

She turned to see Henry standing next to her. She had never seen him in anything but his work uniform or blue jeans, but now he was dressed to the nines in a tuxedo and tie, looking more handsome than she had ever imagined.

"Henry," she managed to say around a mouthful of food.

"Yep, that's me," he said, giving her his perfect smirk and leaning forward to brush a smudge of pie from the corner of her mouth.

"But what are you doing here?" she asked, flushed with excitement.

He laughed. "Well, I'm not quite sure. It seems your sister asked your cousin if I could crash the party."

"My sister?" she asked, confused.

"Your sister Emma asked me if I would like to be your plus-one. I, of course, accepted. Although, I do have to tell you, rustling up a tuxedo on three hours' notice was not an easy feat!"

Catherine felt she would burst with joy. She reached over and gave him a huge hug and a kiss on the cheek.

"Totally worth it, though," he said dreamily, as he

leaned in to kiss her back.

"I thought you might be mad at me for leaving without you last night. I hope you know it wasn't my fault. It's just you weren't there and Thorpe showed up, and he wouldn't listen and he pulled me in, and I would have waited all night for you if I could have..." Catherine stopped speaking, realizing she was just rambling.

Henry said, "I never thought for one moment that you would have left me behind for Thorpe. I mean, not to sound conceited, but I kind of guessed you liked me better. I also heard you have a mean right hook." A grin now spread across his face.

"Well, he did ask for it," she said, smiling back.

"Good to know and remind me to never get on your bad side. So, what's next?" he asked her.

"Oh, I think we will head to our table for dinner," she replied quickly.

"No, I mean what's next for us? I would really like to take you out, Catherine."

She blushed. "I would like that very much."

His smile widened, "Good, I was hoping you would say that. But no more scary dates! Room 813 cured me of any desire to go anywhere haunted."

Catherine considered this for a minute. "Okay, but I do have one favor to ask of you," and she smiled broadly.

"For you, anything," Henry said as he leaned down to kiss her.

CHAPTER 36

Elizabeth

"You must allow me to tell you how ardently I admire and love you."

- PRIDE AND PREJUDICE

Elizabeth watched as the happy couple cut their beautifully designed triple-layer wedding cake.

She grabbed an extra-large slice and started to make her way back to her sisters. At a nearby table, she saw Darcy's aunt sitting with Mrs. Bertram, who had of course brought her dog.

Ms. de Bourgh appeared to be waving her over. Elizabeth checked over her shoulder to make sure she wasn't waving at someone else. Convinced she was being summoned, she made her way to the table and addressed Mrs. Bertram.

"Such a magical wedding, Mrs. B. I wanted to thank you again for everything you've done for us this week." As she leaned over, Elizabeth noticed that Mrs. Norris was wearing a wedding dress made for dogs. She giggled,

"Mrs. Norris looks very beautiful tonight, too."

"Thank you, dear," Mrs. Bertram said, smiling and petting the dog, who was eyeing Elizabeth's cake.

Elizabeth heard Ms. de Bourgh say, "Sit," and wasn't sure if she was talking to her or the dog.

"You," she said, pointing her fork at Elizabeth, who obliged and pulled out a chair to join them at the table. "What's going on with you and my nephew?" she asked accusingly. Her fork was still pointed in her direction, and then she stuck it into her own piece of cake.

"With Darcy?" Elizabeth asked, confused by the question.

"Don't be coy with me, young lady," snapped Ms. de Bourgh. "He's boring me to death talking about you. 'Elizabeth this and Elizabeth that'—you've bewitched the boy. If your intention is to get hired at Pemberley, you can forget it. I'll never allow it."

Elizabeth gave an exasperated sigh. "Ms. de Bourgh, I have no idea why you think I would ever consider coming to work at Pemberley, but I can assure you I have no such intentions."

"Good. Then we have an understanding." The tension disappeared from the older woman's face.

"Oh, absolutely," replied Elizabeth. "I have my sights set much higher than a job." She delighted in the look of horror on Ms. de Bourgh's face.

When she rose abruptly to leave, she noticed her slice of cake was slightly smaller and a little smudged. She glanced over and saw what appeared to be icing on the nose of Mrs. Norris. As she walked away, she heard Ms. de Bourgh say with indignation, "Such a rude girl. That's what happens when you are raised without manners. Hmph!"

Elizabeth watched as Mrs. Norris climbed back onto the table to eat the rest of the slice of cake she had left behind.

She smiled as she made her way back to her table. So Darcy had been speaking about her to his aunt. What did that mean, and why did it give her butterflies?

When she arrived back at the table, all her sisters were gone. She sat down, then looked up, startled to see Darcy standing at the table.

"Mind if I join you?" he said, holding two plates, a slice of cake on each. He set one down in front of her and took a seat.

"I saw you talking with my aunt," he said shyly.

Elizabeth smiled. "Yeah, I think she really likes me."

Darcy laughed at this, and she noticed how his whole demeanor changed when he was relaxed. "Don't worry, she doesn't like anyone," he said.

"She likes Caroline," Elizabeth said, clearly fishing for his reaction.

Darcy sighed. "Yes, I know. She would like to see us get together. It's just one more way I am a disappointment to her."

"So, you're not interested in Caroline?" she asked. She tried to sound nonchalant, unable to make eye contact.

"No, Caroline is not the one I'm interested in," he said, and now she looked up and caught his intense gaze. "If I may ask, what about you and Wickham? Things didn't work out? I noticed he's spending a lot of time with Lydia."

"You just want to hear me say you were right, don't you?" she asked teasingly and gave his arm a playful nudge. Even that little bit of contact sent a shiver up her.

He smiled. "I'm just glad you figured him out on your own." He fidgeted in his seat as though he were uncomfortable. "Listen, Elizabeth, I know we didn't get off on the right foot, and I'll understand if you feel nothing's changed, but I would like to try again. Will you have dinner with me when we get home?"

Elizabeth felt her heart soar. Somewhere along the way, she had fallen for him. She wasn't sure when or how it had happened, but now she knew. She liked Darcy, really liked him. She never would have guessed it was possible after that first disastrous date, and yet she knew she couldn't wait to go out with him again.

"I can't tell from your face if that's a yes or a no," he said with a look of concern.

Elizabeth inched her chair a little closer to Darcy. "I don't know, rich men aren't really my type," she said, smiling up at him mischievously. She watched as a smile lit up his entire face again.

"Well, that's a shame, because headstrong, obstinate women are very much my type," he said in a husky murmur.

"Oh, big word, 'obstinate.' Sounds a bit pretentious."

"I've been told that's a fault of mine."

"We will just have to work on that."

"So that's a yes, then?" he asked.

She smiled up at him. "It's a yes," she said. "Definitely a yes!"

His whole face relaxed, and his broad smile lit up his eyes. "Great, that's great!"

She reached out for his hand and said, "I don't think we should waste any more of this gorgeous evening. Let's go dance."

He hesitated. "I don't know about that. I don't dance."

She gave him her irresistible smile and tugged him out of his seat. "Well, no time like the present to start practicing! If you are going to date me, you're going to have to learn."

Darcy let her lead him to the dance floor. He gazed down at her and whispered, "Has anyone ever told you that you have the most beautiful eyes?"

She looked up at him adoringly. "You're just trying to

distract me so you don't have to dance," she laughed.

"Is it working?" he asked, holding his gaze on hers for a long moment. He brushed a soft, lingering kiss against her lips. Then he pulled her in even closer with a kiss more passionate and certain.

Elizabeth forgot all about dancing.

CHAPTER 37

Anne

"Let us never underestimate the power of a well-written letter."

- PERSUASION

Anne dreamily stared out onto the dance floor, watching Catherine and Elizabeth dance with their dates. She was pretty sure Elizabeth's partner was the man she had told them about earlier this morning. She looked at Elizabeth's face, which was looking up adoringly at her date.

Anne smiled. Whatever she may have felt for him before, it was obvious something had changed her mind.

She sighed and looked around the pavilion for Frederick. During the ceremony, she had spotted him sitting among the guests, but she hadn't seen him since. She tried to conceal her disappointment. Tonight was her last opportunity to talk with him, and she wanted to share all the feelings that were bottled up inside her.

Elinor slid into the seat next to her. "You look so lonesome sitting here all by yourself," she said, nudging

Anne's shoulder.

Anne gave her a wistful smile. "Weddings make me happy and sad at the same time."

Elinor looked at her with a gleam in her eye. "I want to show you something." She pulled out her phone, and Anne watched as Elinor opened up Emma's dating app.

"Don't tell me you actually posted in Em's app?" she asked incredulously.

Elinor scoffed. "Not quite, but I did open it to see how it was going. I think you should take a look."

Anne took the phone from Elinor and looked down at Emma's app. It appeared to be getting some traction and was starting to fill up with profiles and posts. She scrolled past profiles of men and women discussing where they would like to have their ideal date, as well as pics of couples who'd posted after successful dates. She smiled when she saw Catherine and Henry smiling, a horse-drawn carriage in the background.

"Oh, this is going to make Emma so happy," Anne said. "Maybe we have been a little hard on her. She really is onto something with this. It looks like it could be pretty popular." She started to hand the phone back to Elinor, but Elinor pushed it back toward her.

"Keep scrolling," she said with a mischievous smile on her face. Anne looked back down at the phone and continued to look through the posts. Then she stopped, startled at the face smiling back at her. Was that Freddy? He had created a profile on Emma's app?

She looked back up at Elinor, who now had a huge smile on her face. "Read it, you goof!" Anne looked back down and started to read what Freddy had posted.

I can wait no longer and can only hope these words reach you. I am looking for the girl who stole my heart and asking her for a second chance. For these seven years past, I have loved no other. My soul has been only half mine, as you hold the other piece. You once asked me for forgiveness, but I am the one who asks for it now. If you can forgive me, meet me at Mansfield Gardens Lake at 10 p.m. tonight, June 14th. I will wait in agony, uncertain of my fate but full of hope.

Anne read and reread it, the words hardly making sense. She looked at Elinor. "This is for me," she whispered.

Elinor nodded and took her hand. "Yes, I'm guessing it is. I think you have a date to go meet." Anne checked the time. It was a quarter to 10:00. "You have just enough time to get down to the lake," said Elinor.

Anne stood up. Her legs felt wobbly beneath her. She turned to Elinor. "I better go." She reached over and gave her sister a hug. "Wait, when did you see this? How did you know to tell me?"

Elinor gave her a smile and said, "I think Emma might have had something to do with it."

Anne squeezed her sister's hand and rushed toward the lake. Her heart was beating outside her chest as she looked over toward the folly that sat next to the lake. She saw the outline of someone standing there and knew in an instant that it was him. As she got closer, she saw that he was waiting for her, a big smile across his face.

"You came," he said, running his hand through his hair and looking nervous.

"Was there any doubt?" she whispered back.

He came forward and took both of her hands in his. "Anne, how can you ask that?" The agony in his voice shook Anne to her bones. "After you refused my proposal, I was so hurt. You had always been my lifeline. With you, I was always braver. Without you, I was lost. I thought about coming back for you, but I heard through mutual friends that you were doing well, thriving in college, and I knew I couldn't put myself through another rejection." He was looking at her with such sorrowful eyes that Anne felt her heart would burst.

She felt her own eyes fill with tears. "I have regretted saying no every day since. And I never, *ever*, once forgot about you," she said, choking back a sob.

"Should we try this again?" he said, getting down on one knee. He pulled a small box from his pocket and opened it to reveal a ring. "Anne Austen, will you do me the honor of being my wife?"

Anne could hardly see through the tears, but she gave him an emphatic nod and held out her hand.

"Is that a yes?" he asked as he laughed and smiled up at her.

"Oh, it's definitely a yes!" she said with absolute joy. Frederick slid the ring onto her finger. Then he stood up, cupped her face with his hands, and leaned forward to passionately kiss her, the love of his life.

As if on cue, fireworks exploded above their heads out over the lake. "Did you plan those too?" she asked in amazement, gazing up at the bursts of color lighting up the sky.

Frederick laughed. "I wish I could take credit for that, but I think those are for Fanny and Edmund." He bent down and lightly brushed his lips to hers, then her nose, then her brow. And then kissed her lips again, and again, and again.

Chapter 38

Emma

"Faultless, in spite of her faults."

\- Emma

Emma smiled with satisfaction as she watched Anne and Frederick head back to the wedding tent hand in hand.

"What are you smiling at?" She heard the voice of George Knightley as he sat down in the seat next to her.

"And you said I was no matchmaker," she replied, nodding toward Anne and Frederick.

He grinned back at her. "Nicely done, Emma."

"Now that I see them together, I don't know how I didn't see it sooner," she said. "They seem made for each other, don't they?"

"Please tell me after this your matchmaking days are coming to an end," he moaned.

Emma laughed. "What, and quit while I'm ahead? Never!"

"And how is it that the beautiful Emma Austen finds herself sitting alone at a wedding?" he asked with genuine curiosity, and she again noticed the intensity of his blue eyes.

"Well, technically I'm not alone. You're here!" she said, holding his gaze.

"I confess, I came with an ulterior motive."

Emma felt her pulse quicken. This was the second time she and Knightley had been this close, and she wondered why he gave her butterflies. Was he about to ask her out? Did she want him to? She wasn't sure if she knew the answer to that.

Knightley continued, "I was really impressed with what you did for Fanny and Edmund. How you managed to pull off such a wonderful event on no notice and make it look effortless. I think you have a real talent, and, well…I was wondering if you would consider coming to work for me. My family owns several resorts, and we could use an event planner, someone who isn't just media savvy but has the eye and the talent to pull off the decor. I think you would be perfect."

Emma couldn't hide the surprise in her voice. "Are you offering me a job?"

Knightley laughed. "Yes, I am."

Emma tried to absorb what this would entail. She loved what she had accomplished on social media, but this didn't mean she would have to give it up. In fact, it could be the perfect chance to grow her following while also providing a more stable income.

She looked back at Knightley. "I accept," she said without a second thought.

He smiled broadly. "I hoped you would. I think I'm going to like having you around."

"Who knows, maybe I'll find the perfect match for you," she said teasingly.

He stood up to leave and gave her a steady glance. "Oh, you'll have no luck there. I already have someone in mind," he said.

Emma felt a pang of disappointment, which surprised her.

"I've had my eye on someone for a long time. I was just waiting for her to grow up." He gave her his biggest smile and walked off.

Emma sat there stunned as she watched him walk away.

She was still sitting there, smiling dreamily, when Anne and Frederick approached. Anne ran up to her and hugged her sister tight.

"Oh, Emma, I know I have you to thank for my happiness!" Tears formed in her eyes. "Look," she said, extending her hand, which was now adorned with a large diamond. "Frederick and I are engaged!"

Emma stood up and hugged them both. "I'm so happy for you, Anne," she said, and her heart filled with joy for her sister.

"We have to go find the others! Don't tell them if you see them first," Anne said, beaming with happiness.

She started to walk away, and then she turned back to Emma. "Have you checked your app lately?" she said with a coy smile. "If not, you might want to."

It occurred to Emma that not only had she not checked her dating app, she hadn't even been on her phone most of the evening. She had enjoyed being in the moment for once, not worried about capturing the perfect picture or post.

She picked up her phone and opened the app with curiosity. She saw the perfect selfie of Anne and Frederick. They had taken a picture down by the lake, with the dim glow of the wedding lights in the background and fireworks above their heads.

The caption read, *Best date ever, Mansfield Park Gardens and Lake…I said yes!*

It already had hundreds of likes and comments about

how it was the perfect spot for a proposal, engagement pics, or a wedding. Emma kept scrolling. Her feed was full of posts.

She stopped suddenly when she saw a picture of Catherine and Henry standing in a long hallway with a hotel room behind them.

The perfect date for those who love a hauntingly good time! Mansfield Park Room 813...enter at your own risk!

She giggled at her sister and Henry's pretend scared faces. She was just getting ready to close the app when one last picture caught her attention.

It was Elizabeth with the tall, grumpy guy she had told them about earlier today. They, too, had snapped a selfie, this one in front of a book-lined shelf with a fireplace in the background. *A book lover's dream date, Mansfield Park Library...Reader, I'm dating him.*

Emma felt a surge of love and gratitude for her sisters. She had set things right, and she had been forgiven.

CHAPTER 39

Elinor

*"I come here with no expectations, only to profess, now that
I am at liberty to do so, that my heart is and always will be...
yours."*

- SENSE AND SENSIBILITY

The morning had been bittersweet as Elinor said
her goodbyes. It had been a big week. Fanny was
now Mrs. Bertram, Emma had a new job, Elizabeth and
Catherine had new boyfriends, and Anne was engaged.
She was over the moon for all of them, but she felt a sense
of sadness at heading back to her busy, lonely life. She
wanted to see Eddie, but she dreaded what it would mean
for their friendship. It felt like her sisters were moving
forward, but she was stuck in the same place.

She looked down at her watch and realized she was
running late for her flight. She rushed through the airport,
practically sprinting to her gate. All the excitement of the
morning had made her late leaving Mansfield, and now
she was cutting it close to missing her flight.

She couldn't help but laugh to herself. She was now one

of *those* people. She sighed a breath of relief as she spied the gate and saw the last group of people still boarding the plane. She filed in behind them, had her boarding pass scanned, and stepped onto the jetway. Maybe this wasn't so bad.

If only my sisters could see me now, practically the last one on the plane, she thought. She smiled at the flight attendant and looked down for her seat designation. 18B. *Damn, the middle seat again*, and she groaned. Next time, she would have to pay more attention to her seat assignment when she booked.

She shoved her luggage into the overhead and took her seat in the middle. She glanced over at the elderly gentleman sitting in the window seat, his face covered with a mask. He seemed distracted and was mumbling to himself as he searched through his carry-on bag.

Elinor tried to relax, but the gentleman's fidgeting was making her uneasy. She watched as he hit the call button for the flight attendant, who appeared rather quickly.

"Yes, Mr. Woodhouse, what can I do for you now?" Her tone was exasperated. It was clear this was not the first time she had been summoned to his seat.

"I'm feeling a draft," he said, his manner agitated and his voice rising. "I'm susceptible to the cold—I can't catch a cold at my age. Do you feel the draft?" he asked, looking over at Elinor.

She groaned inwardly but gave him a sympathetic smile. "Would you like me to trade places with you?" Elinor offered, hopeful he would be willing to switch seats.

"No, no, that won't do. I can't be around too many people."

The exasperated attendant tried again. "Mr. Woodhouse, sir, you are on a plane. There are going to be people and drafts. Now, I can bring you a blanket, or you can trade places with this kind young woman, but those are really your only options." She sighed with a look of boredom.

"Fine, I'll take the blanket. Better make it two, and a pillow," he replied begrudgingly.

Elinor sighed. It was going to be another long flight.

She opened her phone to send one last text to her sisters. As she typed, she felt someone slide into the aisle seat.

"Excuse me, I need to reach for my seat belt," she heard him say. There was something familiar about the voice. She looked up.

His dark eyes met hers, and he smiled the biggest smile and said, "Hello, Elinor."

Eddie. It was Eddie. Sitting beside her on the plane. Her mind couldn't quite grasp it. Why was he in Kentucky? What was he doing on her plane? It couldn't be a coincidence.

She felt breathless as she said, "Eddie, I don't understand—what are you doing here?" She could barely get the words out.

He reached out and took her hand, clasping it tight in his own. Elinor felt a jolt of electricity go through her.

"I don't think I'm very good at what they call 'the grand gesture,'" he said, a bemused smile on his face.

"The grand gesture?" Elinor repeated, still confused and finding it hard to believe that Eddie was here next to her.

"Yes. Your sister Elizabeth told me all good romances have a grand gesture. You know, where the lover runs to stop the flight or makes a fool of himself in front of strangers. I had mine all planned. I was going to show up at the wedding yesterday, but my flight was delayed, and then it was too late. By the time I got there this morning, your sisters told me you were gone. So, here I am."

He leaned closer to her. "You have no idea what it took to arrange this seat. Luckily, the flight attendant is a sucker for romances."

Elinor felt her emotions take over, and the tears started to slip down her face. She tried to regain control. "I don't understand. I thought you were marrying Lucy. How...I mean, why...why are you here?"

He looked across her and out the window, seemingly trying to compose himself. Elinor had not even realized the plane had taken off, and they were now in the air. He looked back at her and sighed.

"I was never in love with Lucy. It was our parents who arranged our engagement. We were both so young; we didn't question it. I didn't know a thing about love. I knew Lucy would be a good wife, and so I went along with it. But the more time I spent with you, the more I began to question everything. I didn't realize I had made a mistake until I met you, Elinor."

She felt a sob escape her throat and struggled for composure.

He took a shaky breath and continued, "I think Lucy started to suspect I was having second thoughts. Then she met Robert, and she started to have doubts of her own. We went to our parents together to break off the engagement, but it didn't go well," he sighed. "They put a lot of pressure on both of us, and we backed off. I'm sure you felt my behavior was odd. I thought I was free, and then I wasn't. I never meant to give you mixed signals."

He grabbed her hand and raised it to his lips. "I am so sorry. Right after you left, Lucy came to me and told me that Robert had proposed, and that, against her family's wishes, she was going to accept. I didn't call you those first few days because the fallout with our family was very dramatic. But they finally came to accept it." He paused for a moment, searching her eyes before continuing. "Lucy was the one who told me to call you and share my feelings. I had no expectation that you felt the same. I was going to wait until you came home to speak with you in person, but then I realized, now that I was free, I couldn't wait any longer. So, I reached out to your sister, Elizabeth, and when she told me how you had seen Lucy's post and how upset you were, well, I had all the hope I needed. I booked the first flight out, but the storms caused cancellations and delays, and well…here I am, flying back home with you."

The tears were now running freely down her face. "I love you," she said through a choking sob. He leaned over and wiped the tears away gently with the brush of his thumb.

"I love you too, Elinor Austen. Now let's go home."

*"My characters shall have, after a little trouble,
all that they desire."*

– JANE AUSTEN

ACKNOWLEDGMENTS

I am deeply grateful to all of the amazing individuals below, without whom this story might never have made it to publication.

To all my early beta readers, a heartfelt thank you for all your positive and enthusiastic feedback. Your support kept me going through moments of doubt and your insights and suggestions were invaluable in shaping my story. Thank you, Emma Heiting, Jennifer Valencia, Melissa Garcia, Teresa Garcia, Bridgitte Binder, Mary Broussard, Ruth Mitchell and Charlie.

A huge thank you to my work crew who were the very first to encourage me and planted the seed that this was something I should pursue. Teresa Garcia, for all your pep talks and brainstorming, your ideas helped make this book better. Bridgitte Binder, for being one of the first to tell me you loved it and for being my very first editor. Ignacio Zavala, for giving me the confidence to start on this journey and all your advice along the way. Andy Lumsden and Saul Silva for cheering me on and enduring countless lunches learning way more about Jane Austen then you ever wanted to know.

Special thanks to Charlie for commenting on almost every page and making me laugh with your notes and observations. You are a gem and a true Janeite!

Emma Heiting, I'm so in love with my cover! Thank you for bringing my vision of the sisters to life with your beautiful illustration. Your drawings kept me motivated when the doubts kicked in.

Ruth Mitchell, I'm so grateful for all your advice and for the generosity with your time to help me navigate this complicated world of publishing a book. You are simply the best!

Thank you, Caroline Knecht and Shannon Cave for cleaning up my manuscript and making it presentable. Thank you, Andrea Purdie for my beautiful cover design.

Finally, with gratitude and love, to my family for all their support helping me chase this dream. My daughter, Katie for reading ALL my drafts, fixing grammar, correcting every double space after a period and listening to me talk nonstop about these characters. My son, Jack, for keeping it real by walking in asking "what's for dinner?" when I was in author mode.

And for my husband, David, thank you for EVERYTHING, I love you, most ardently.